DUMB AND DEAD

Law pulled out the long-barreled .45-caliber Colt Peacemaker and swiftly checked it. He stepped out from behind the house and took a few steps toward the trouble spot.

"That'll be enough of that foolishness, boys," Law said, voice booming.

"Who the hell're you?" the horseman asked.

Law took him to be the leader. "John Thomas Law," he said.

"The bounty man?" the leader questioned.

"The same." Law calmly surveyed the three men. All had the look of outlaws and hard cases, the look of men who had little regard for someone's life or person.

"Well, this ain't none of your affair," the leader said.

"I beg to differ." He paused. "Now you skunks can either ride on out of here or—"

"Or what?" Blue Shirt asked. He had never heard of J.T. Law and was unafraid of him, especially seeing how the odds were three to one against the bounty hunter.

"Or die, you dumb puke," Law snapped.

Blue Shirt went for his pistol.

Law did not hesitate. He raised his Colt and fired twice, drilling Blue Shirt in the heart and head. Not waiting to see Blue Shirt fall, Law swung a bit to his left and kept firing . . .

JUSTICE IN
BIG SPRING

TOM CALHOUN

JOVE BOOKS, NEW YORK

THE BERKLEY PUBLISHING GROUP
Published by the Penguin Group
Penguin Group (USA) Inc.
375 Hudson Street, New York, New York 10014, USA
Penguin Group (Canada), 10 Alcorn Avenue, Toronto, Ontario M4V 3B2, Canada
(a division of Pearson Penguin Canada Inc.)
Penguin Books Ltd., 80 Strand, London WC2R 0RL, England
Penguin Group Ireland, 25 St. Stephen's Green, Dublin 2, Ireland
(a division of Penguin Books Ltd.)
Penguin Group (Australia), 250 Camberwell Road, Camberwell, Victoria 3124,
Australia (a division of Pearson Australia Group Pty. Ltd.)
Penguin Books India Pvt. Ltd., 11 Community Centre, Panchsheel Park, New Delhi—
100 017, India
Penguin Group (NZ), Cnr. Airborne and Rosedale Roads, Albany, Auckland 1310, New
Zealand (a division of Pearson New Zealand Ltd.)
Penguin Books (South Africa) (Pty.) Ltd., 24 Sturdee Avenue, Rosebank,
Johannesburg 2196, South Africa

Penguin Books Ltd., Registered Offices: 80 Strand, London WC2R 0RL, England

JUSTICE IN BIG SPRING

A Jove Book / published by arrangement with the author.

PRINTING HISTORY
Jove edition / November 2004

Copyright © 2004 by The Berkley Publishing Group.
Cover design by Steven Ferlauto.
Cover illustration by Cook.

ISBN: 0-515-13850-9

JOVE®
Jove Books are published by The Berkley Publishing Group,
a division of Penguin Group (USA) Inc.
375 Hudson Street, New York, New York 10014.
JOVE is a registered trademark of Penguin Group (USA) Inc.
The "J" design is a trademark belonging to Penguin Group (USA) Inc.

PRINTED IN THE UNITED STATES OF AMERICA

10 9 8 7 6 5 4 3 2 1

CHAPTER 1

JOHN THOMAS LAW usually skirted farms and ranches when traveling. The bounty hunter had long ago learned that many people living in isolated circumstances were not fond of his sort coming to visit. Besides, he rarely, if ever, had any reason to call at such places. But his trip up from San Angelo, heading toward Big Spring, had been hot and dusty, and the thought of a brief stop at the farm he could see down the rise and half a mile across the prairie was inviting.

He took off his black, low-crowned hat and wiped a shirt-sleeve across his forehead, sopping up sweat. Putting his hat back on, he reached behind him for the short frock coat loosely tied atop his bedroll. It was too hot to wear it, but he figured it wise to cover the long-barreled Colt Peacemaker in the hip holster and the short-barreled one in the shoulder rig. It would, he hoped, ease the farm family's mind about his approach. He tugged the black garment on, then patted the big buckskin horse on the neck. "We'll have us some cool, fresh water right off, Toby," he said. "And I bet they'll have some fresh hay for you."

He clucked to the horse and moved slowly down the rise.

Law stopped several yards from the house—a fairly well-made, though small, plain plank structure with a window several feet to each side of the door. The windows had no glass but were covered by thin oiled paper. A small pen to one side of the house held a chicken coop and a bunch of clucking chickens. Another slightly larger pen on the other side housed two pigs. Law assumed there was a garden patch out back of the house.

"Hello the house," he called, staying in the saddle.

A moment later, a woman came out of the house. She looked wary but open. She was a plain though not unattractive woman who, despite not yet being thirty, Law guessed, showed signs of this hard frontier life on her face. She was dressed simply in a dull brown dress that covered her from neck to ground under a darker brown apron. Mousy brown hair was done up in a bun, which was losing its grip on her tresses.

She had a child of perhaps two on her hip, held there by her left hand and arm, and Law could see a couple of slightly older children peeking out of the partly open door behind her.

"Afternoon, ma'am," Law said, resting his hands on the saddle horn.

"Afternoon." She was still wary, for which Law could not blame her.

"Me and Toby here," he patted the horse's neck again, and was rewarded by a shake of the head and the clink of the metal bit, "are comin' from San Angelo, headin' for Big Spring. And, to tell true, ma'am, it's some mighty hot. I was wonderin' if you had some water to spare for me to fill my canteen and let Toby have a drink. He could also use some hay—or, better, grain, if you got any."

Knowing how tight hard-cash money could be on a farm out in the middle of nowhere like this, he added, "I'm willin' to pay for anything we use."

The woman looked up at him, shading her eyes against the sun with her right hand, thinking. While he was a big man—six foot two or so, she judged, and maybe two hundred pounds, with broad shoulders—and had a hard look about his face, he seemed to exude an aura of calm that left her feeling more comfortable than she usually would be around a tough-looking stranger. His black frock coat, hat, and trousers were coated with trail dust, as was his face. What she could see of his shirt under the coat and vest was once white but now grayish with dirt.

But what drew her attention most was when he removed his hat, lifting the shadow from his piercing blue green eyes. She almost shuddered with a sudden gush of desire, which, thankfully, as far as she was concerned, disappeared almost as fast as it had arisen.

Sensing some hesitancy, which was to be expected, Law said, "If your husband's out in the fields and you want to send one of the young'uns to fetch him, I'll wait."

The woman watched him for a few more moments, then nodded, finally. "Well's over yonder," she said, pointing. "Plenty of hay in the barn. A little grain, too, though not much. We don't have much call for it with just the work mules and one ol' horse."

"Much obliged, ma'am," Law said, slapping his hat back on. "Toby'll be sparin' in what he eats."

"No need for that, mister. That seems to be a fine animal, and deserves the best. You take what you need now, ya hear."

"Yes'm." He turned Toby's head and allowed the horse to walk to the well. Law dismounted and cranked a bucket of water up. Using the ladle that hung from a peg pounded into the frame of the well crank, he sipped some of the cool liquid. He hung the ladle back up and then held the bucket out to where Toby could get to it.

As the horse drank, Law said, "Right now that's even better than the finest whiskey back at the Manor House, ain't that right, boy?" He smiled as the horse ignored him. He wished he was in the Manor House now. It was the finest hotel in Austin, and the place he usually stayed when he was there. It was as close as anything Law had to a home or headquarters.

Law dropped the bucket into the well with a splash and cranked it up again, letting Toby drink some more. He had hoped to make Big Spring by nightfall or shortly after, but by the looks of it, that was not going to happen, and he faced another night out in the open. He was tired of sleeping on the ground and eating his own cooking. He'd pay prime for a soft bed, a good, home-cooked meal. And a woman. That would be the topper.

He sighed, knowing none of that was going to happen, at least not tonight, and set the bucket on the well. Then, Toby's reins in hand, he headed for the barn, noticing one of the children, who had been inside of the house, running across the prairie behind the house. Law figured he was going to get his father.

The barn's dimness was a great relief after the relentless sun and the heat it brought. He unsaddled and unbridled Toby, giving the horse a breather. Then, with a short search, Law found a burlap sack of grain and poured a goodly portion of it into a feed trough. While Toby ate, Law walked to the barn door and leaned against the jamb. He pulled out a thin cigar and fired it up. As he blew out a stream of smoke, he watched a man heading toward him.

The man was of medium height but substantially broad, with wide shoulders and an impressive belly hanging over the top of well-worn pants of an indeterminate color. On his head was a battered, floppy slouch hat full of holes and the same indeterminate color as his trousers. The hat kept his face in shadow until he had stopped in front of Law.

"Name's Cletus Honegger," he said, thrusting out a hand.

"John Thomas Law." He took the hand, a hard lump of callus and muscle. He was a little surprised but relieved that Honegger had shown no sign of recognition of his name. Many people knew him by reputation, which was both an asset and a drawback. There were times that having the reputation as a hard case made his job easier. But there were times when it was nothing more than a nuisance, creating fear and worry in people who had no reason to be frightened of him.

Honegger looked Law up and down, then stared into his eyes. Apparently seeing what he wanted to see, he nodded. "You find the grain all right?" he asked.

Law nodded. "I'm obliged. How much I owe you?"

"No need for money, Mr. Law," Honegger said.

Law smiled a bit, taking in the farmer's full, rumpled face, one full of character. "I ain't much given to takin' handouts, Mr. Honegger," he said. "You work hard for what you have, and there ain't really a reason for you to go givin' it out to some stranger."

"We don't get many strangers here, Mr. Law," Honegger said. "It's the least we can do."

"At least let me pay you a little something for the grain. That ain't easy to come by."

"All right," Honegger said hesitantly. He could use any extra cash he could get his hands on, but he did not feel comfortable asking for money from someone who had just wandered by and needed help. "Fifty cent ought to be more than enough."

Law reached into a frock pocket and pulled out a silver dollar. He handed it to Honegger. "You keep that, Mr. Honegger. It's fair for what I took."

Honegger nodded, offering a shy smile. "It'll be put to good use, Mr. Law."

"I wager it will," Law agreed. He blew out a stream of cigar smoke toward the blazing blue sky.

"Well, I best get back to work," Honegger said.

Law nodded. "I should be back on the trail before long. Soon's Toby there finishes feedin' and I get him saddled up again, we'll be on our way,"

"No need to hurry." Honegger turned and shuffled away.

Law dropped his cigar in the dirt and ground it out with the toe of his boot. Then he turned and went back inside the barn. Toby had finished the grain and seemed to be casting about for more, so Law poured an extra helping into the trough.

While he stood there watching the horse eat, Law thought he heard riders approaching. It seemed curious after Honegger saying that the farm had few strangers come by. He supposed it could be neighbors, though considering the distances between farms, that seemed unlikely. He patted the horse's flank and moved toward the door, where he stopped just inside it and peered out.

Three men sat on horseback in front of the house about where Law had been not long ago. Honegger stood in front of them, arms across his ample chest. His wife was right behind him. Law could not see her face, of course, from this distance, but he was certain it would be showing defiance. The children were not to be seen, and Law figured they were inside the house. He could not hear what was being said, but from long experience and the way they were all acting, he suspected that trouble was brewing.

He hurried back inside and made sure Toby was secured with a simple rope hobble, then headed outside, around the far end of the barn to the back. He scooted across the open ground behind the chicken pen to the back of the house. There was, as he had expected, a garden patch there. He slipped around the corner of the house and began moving up along the wall between the house and the pigpen. As he reached the front corner, he heard a shot, and he peeked out.

Honegger lay on the ground. Two of the three men had dismounted and were moving toward the woman. Those two and their companion were laughing. The man on the horse still held a smoking pistol in his hand.

One of the men—clad in a blue shirt under a leather vest— grabbed Mrs. Honegger, who struggled but could do little against the larger, far stronger man. Another—also wearing a blue shirt, but no vest—grabbed her dress front and yanked. "Let's see what you got there under that ol' dress, sweetheart," he said, a leer in his voice. The dress refused to yield.

Law pulled out the long-barreled .45-caliber Colt Peacemaker and swiftly checked it. With it in hand, held down alongside his thigh, he stepped out from behind the house and took a few steps toward the trouble spot.

"That'll be enough of that foolishness, boys," Law said, voice booming.

Blue Shirt whirled, Leather Vest looked up sharply, though he did not let go of Mrs. Honegger, and the man on horseback snapped his head toward Law.

"Who the hell're you?" the horseman asked in a voice that had a small but unmistakable quaver.

Law took him to be the leader. "John Thomas Law," he said.

"The bounty man?" Leader questioned.

"The same." Law calmly surveyed the three men. All had the look of outlaws and hard cases, the look of men who had little regard for someone's life or person.

"Well, this here ain't none of your affair," the leader said with bravado.

"I beg to differ, pard." He paused, looking from one man to the other. "Now you skunks got a choice here. You can either ride on out of here now or—"

"Or what?" Blue Shirt asked. He had never heard of J.T. Law and was unafraid of him, especially seeing as how the odds were three to one against the bounty hunter.

"Or die, you dumb puke," Law snapped.

Blue Shirt threw back his head and laughed for a few moments. Then he stopped and went for his pistol.

Law did not hesitate. He raised his Colt and fired twice, drilling Blue Shirt in the heart and head. Blue Shirt hit the dirt, bloody and dead, before he had even managed to pull his Remington.

Not waiting to see Blue Shirt fall, Law swung a bit to his left and fired twice at the leader. He knew he hit the man at least once, but whether he had killed him or if the leader had just fallen or jumped off his horse was unknown.

Law swung back. Leather Vest was having trouble holding on to Mrs. Honegger with one hand while trying to unlimber his revolver, but he finally managed to do so. Before he could bring it to bear on Law, Mrs. Honegger screamed, "No!" Then she kicked him in the shin with a heel.

Leather Vest yelped as Mrs. Honegger jerked free and darted out of the way. He was bringing his pistol up to shoot at Law, when the bounty man plugged him twice in the chest, sending him reeling backward, where he tripped over Honegger and fell, dead.

Mrs. Honegger ran there, crying and screaming, and shoved Leather Vest off her husband, whom she cradled to her bosom.

Law dropped the big Peacemaker into the tied-down holster on his right hip. A moment after he drew the smaller version of the revolver from the shoulder holster, the leader came walking slowly around the back of the horses. He was grinning.

"Looks like you're shit out of luck, bounty man," the man said, stopping a few feet from Law.

Not betraying any of his bemusement, Law simply asked, "What's your name, boy?"

The man seemed surprised. "Wally Corwin," he finally said. "Why?"

"Well, I never had the opportunity with your two damfool friends over there, but I like to know the name of the men I'm about to kill."

Corwin laughed. "You got balls, Law, I'll say that. I've always heard that, but like most stories, I figured it was at least half bullshit." He paused, still grinning. "You got any last words?"

CHAPTER 2

✦

"Yes, I do," Law said. "Good-bye, asswipe." He jerked the pistol up and shot Corwin three times.

Corwin, face registering as much surprise as pain, gaped at Law for a moment before falling in a heap in the dirt. "How?" he asked, voice barely more than a whisper, when Law walked up to stand over him.

Law pulled back the left side of his frock coat, revealing the empty shoulder holster. "Second piece," he said flatly.

Corwin's eyes widened, then he gave a shuddering breath and died.

Law bent and took Corwin's gun and flung it away, just in case. Then he rose and reloaded the small Colt, returned it to the holster, and did the same with the larger Peacemaker. He turned and headed toward the Honeggers. As he knelt by them, he was startled—and relieved—to see that Honegger was alive. The bullet had hit him in the shoulder.

"Let's get him inside, ma'am," Law said with a new sense of urgency. "I don't think he's hurt too bad."

"I ain't," Honegger commented, wincing a little with the

pain. With Law's help, he got to his feet, and the bounty man helped him inside and onto the bed in the small bedroom at the back of the house.

Law cut Honegger's shirt off and, while holding him up in a sitting position, checked the wound front and back. "It ain't so bad," he said. "Bullet went clean through and didn't hit any bone or anything. A few weeks and he'll be right as rain."

"You sure?" Mrs. Honegger asked, face and light brown eyes reflecting her worry.

"Yes'm," Law allowed.

"But . . ."

"Now, Vera, don't get yourself all worked up frettin' over me," Honegger said. The words were a little harsh, perhaps, but there was a loving gentleness in his tone.

"Go and fetch some bandaging material, ma'am," Law said quietly. When she had done so, along with some hot water to clean the wound, he asked, "Will you be able to handle the doctorin' by yourself?"

Vera Honegger nodded, her manner now businesslike. She had pushed down her fear and worry, not wanting to look weak in front of her husband and this tall, handsome stranger. Nor did she want to spread her worry to her children, who had gathered around.

Law felt a bit uncomfortable around the five children, not counting the smallest, whom Mrs. Honegger had placed in a rudimentary crib—boys of about fifteen, twelve, and eight; girls of ten and six. Law was not used to being around so many youngsters all at once, and he was eager to get away from them.

"I'll be back in a spell," Law said, heading outside. He walked to the barn and searched a bit until he found some sheets of canvas. He carried them back to where the bodies of Corwin and his two companions lay. He dropped the canvas and then went through the men's pockets. He came up with a total of twenty-eight dollars and fifty-seven cents. There was little else of value—three penknives and a pair of watches, neither of them worth much. He left the watches and penknives but stuffed the cash into his coat pocket. He pulled their gun belts off and set them aside.

Taking off his coat, he folded it neatly and set it on the

ground near the door of the house. Then he wrapped each body in canvas, tying the material tightly. He heaved each one in turn onto the back of a horse and lashed it to the saddle.

By the time that was done, he was sweating heavily. He took each man's gun belt and looped it over a saddle horn. Finally he led all three horses into the barn, out of the sun. He went back out, straight to the nearby well and not only drank his fill but poured some of the cool water over his head, face, and neck. It served to revive him a bit.

Back in the barn, he saddled and bridled Toby. Leaving all the animals there, he went back to the house. He stopped and picked up his coat and put it on after vainly trying to slap some of the dirt and dust off it.

Law entered the house and went straight to the room at back. Honegger was bandaged and, while he looked to be in pain, was alert. Vera still sat on the side of the bed, talking softly to him. She held one of his big paws in her small hands.

"Looks like you're doin' well, Mr. Honegger," Law said with a small smile.

"Ain't so bad, I expect," the farmer responded. "Feels like I been kicked by one of my mules. . . ." He slapped his thigh. "The mules. Little C, you and Jeremy go out to the field and fetch the mules back here to the barn and tend 'em. And make sure the cows're back and milked."

"Yes, Pa," the eldest son said. He and the next oldest boy hurried out.

"Well, Mr. Honegger—"

"Cletus."

Law nodded. "Well, Cletus, it looks like you'll be fine, and you're in good hands." He smiled briefly at Vera. "So I aim to be on my way. It's still a fair piece of ridin' before I get to Big Spring."

"No," Vera exclaimed before her husband could say anything.

Both men looked at her in surprise.

She flushed in embarrassment. "I mean, no, you can't go yet, Mr. Law," she added in a rushed voice. "It's late in the day, and you've had nothing to eat. I insist you stay for supper, and stay the night to be rested for your journey tomorrow."

"That ain't necessary, ma'am," Law allowed.

"Yes, it is," Vera said adamantly. "It's the least we can do for you after what you . . . how you helped us."

"Vera's right," Honegger said with a firm nod. "What you done for us was . . . well, dammit, you saved us both from a mighty unpleasant death." He didn't say that he figured that his wife would have suffered even more before she would have been killed. "And while a meal and a roof for the night ain't really enough of a payin' back for such that we owe you, a meal cooked by Vera is a mighty fine thing."

His wife blushed again at the compliment.

Law didn't have to consider it long, if at all. He would never make Big Spring today, so he would have to spend another night sleeping on the ground and eating his own poorly made food. That did not appeal to him. And there was no reason to rush. He had told his old friend Howard County Sheriff Jesse McCracken that he would be in Big Spring as soon as he could get there. But tomorrow afternoon instead of morning would be soon enough.

He nodded. "I'd be right honored to stay, Cletus, ma'am." He grinned. "I could do with a good meal, and even a bed of straw out in the barn'll be better than another night on the hard ground out there on the prairie."

"I thought you might see the light," Honegger said.

"I best go unsaddle Toby again, though," Law said.

"You'll be back, won't you?" Vera asked.

"Oh, yes, ma'am." He grinned again. Law turned to leave, then turned back. "Oh, I almost forgot this." He pulled the money out of his frock coat pocket and held it out toward the Honeggers.

"Why, you don't need to pay us, Mr. Law," Vera said, looking abashed that he would think such a thing necessary. "It's we who owe you so much." She glanced for just a moment at the handful of paper money and coins. She and her husband could use that money, but she could not take it from Law, who had done so much for them.

The bounty hunter grinned again. "I ain't payin' you for your hospitality, ma'am," he said with a chuckle. "This money belonged to those bast—those boys who sought to do you harm. They got no more use for it, and after what they done to you, you deserve it."

Vera's eyes moved from Law's to the money ever so briefly, then to her husband's. He looked lost in thought, but it lasted only a moment. Then he nodded to his wife. She turned back to the bounty hunter and took the money.

"I don't know what to say, Mr. Law," she whispered. "This'll sure come in handy."

"I figured it would. And, as I said, you deserve it after what they done to Cletus and tried to do to you. I just wish it was a heap more." He winked at Honegger. "I know you folks'll put it to good use." He turned and headed out.

After unsaddling his horse and making sure the outlaws' horses had hay and water, Law went back to the house. "You have somewhere I can wash up?" he asked. "I'd hate to use well water for it, unless there's no other choice."

"There's a rain barrel out round the back of the house," Vera said. "Next to it is a little stand with a basin and a dish of soft soap."

"Obliged." Law went out back, realizing he had not seen the barrel on his dash across the back of the house earlier. He dipped some water into the basin. It was warm water, but it would be fine for washing up. He felt almost like a new man when he headed back into the house, which was now filled with the aroma of simmering chicken and dumplings, fresh buttermilk biscuits, and vanity cakes.

"That sure smells like fine feedin', ma'am," Law said as he took off his hat and hung it on a peg next to the door. He decided it was best to leave his coat on. He sat at one end of the longish, battered wood table, opposite Honegger. "How're you farin', Cletus?" he asked.

"Not so bad," the farmer said evenly.

The pain etched on his face belied his statement, though. Still, Law figured he would eat heartily and probably be back at work in the fields tomorrow, though he would likely take it a bit easy for a few weeks.

"I hope you're hungry, Mr. Law," Vera said as she began setting the table.

"If I wasn't before, I would be now, ma'am," Law responded. "Those smells are right encitin'."

Vera smiled. "You children go on and wash up now," she ordered. "Supper'll be ready directly."

AFTER THE MEAL was done—and a fine meal it was, Law told Vera—the children went off to various chores and Vera began cleaning up. Honegger moved up to sit at right angles to Law. The two sipped coffee, and Law brought out two small cigars, handing one to Honegger. When the cigars were going, Law asked, "You know them fellas who caused that spot of trouble, Cletus?"

"No, sir. Never seen a one of 'em before."

"What'd they want?"

"I ain't sure what they wanted when they first rode up," Honegger said with a shrug that elicited a sharp grimace of pain. "But soon's they saw Vera . . ." His voice and eyes had turned angry.

"I understand, Cletus," Law said soothingly. "No need to fret over it now. I was just wonderin' if there's been trouble with these boys before. Or if there was somethin' else goin' on. Them fellas don't seem none too bright, and such boys usually either work for somebody or get killed young."

"Well, Mr. Law," Honegger allowed, "I don't know how old they were, but they're sure as hell dead." He gave a sidelong glance toward his wife to see if she was bothered by the mild profanity; she often was. But she either hadn't heard it or was pretending not to.

"That they are, Cletus."

Honegger had a sudden thought, and his eyes widened. "What'd you do with those outlaws, Mr. Law?" he asked, worried.

"Call me J.T. Or John Thomas."

Honegger nodded. "You didn't go and bury them out there somewhere did you?" Out of the corner of his eye, he spied Vera watching him and Law.

The bounty man saw the woman watching, too, and he

smiled a bit. "No, Cletus. I'd never presume to do such a thing." He noticed Vera breathe a sigh of relief and go back to scrubbing dishes. "I just rolled 'em up in some canvas I found out in the barn and tied 'em over their horses. I'll cart 'em into Big Spring with me tomorrow." His grin widened. "You never know, there might be a reward on 'em. Though if there is, I reckon it's mighty small."

Vera soon began putting the younger children to bed, and before long, Honegger was looking as if he could use some sleep. The pain of his wound was really getting to him, and it showed. He finally stood. "Well, J.T.," he said heavily, "I reckon I'd best be abed." He looked at his wife, who sat rocking as she sewed a patch onto a shirt. "You think he should have the boys' bed, don't you, Vera?"

She nodded. "After what he's done for us, he should have that little comfort. Little Cletus, Jeremy, and Wally can make do with a night in the barn." She smiled at Law. "Bed's right in there," she added, pointing.

"I'm obliged, ma'am," the bounty hunter said. "But I reckon I'll make my bed in the barn tonight. Those boys don't need to spend the night with some corpses."

The three eldest Honegger boys, all sitting on the floor, resting, looked relieved.

"Good night, folks."

"You'll be here yet for breakfast?" Vera asked. She seemed anxious.

"Yes'm. I wouldn't miss a fine breakfast like you're bound to make, judgin' from the supper you put up not so long ago."

WITH A FULL belly, and more thanks ringing in his ears, John Thomas Law rode out of the Honegger farm, towing three corpse-laden horses behind him. Even at this early hour, it was obvious the day was going to be another scorcher.

He rode slowly but steadily. He didn't want to wear Toby down or abuse the faithful buckskin, but he did not want to spend the whole day on the trail either. Not with three ripening bodies along.

It was shortly after noon when he entered Big Spring, riding slowly down the main street in the sweltering heat, ignoring the curious glances that men, women, and children cast at him. He stopped in front of the county sheriff's office, dismounted, and tied Toby and the three other horses to the hitching rail. As he was finishing, the door to the office opened and Jesse McCracken stepped out. His grin of greeting faded when he saw the three canvas-wrapped bodies.

CHAPTER 3

✶

"Damn, J.T., can't you keep out of trouble just ridin' the trail from one place to another?" McCracken asked.

"Sometimes trouble just rears up and bites a man, Jess," Law allowed. "You ought to know that."

Law and McCracken had fought together with Quantrill and Bloody Bill Anderson. McCracken had been seriously wounded in a savage skirmish with Union regulars up in Kansas and had gone home to Texas to recuperate. Law had seen him only once after that, but Law was too deep in the bottle at the time to remember much about the encounter. All he could recall, and it was fuzzy at that, was that McCracken seemed to be a lawman of a sort, even then.

"Yeah, I do know that," McCracken said seriously. He had seen a lifetime's worth of troubles since the war. And it was, in most ways, why he was what he was today.

"What happened that you come ridin' into Big Spring with three bodies slung over saddles. J.T.?" McCracken asked.

Law explained it briefly, succinctly.

"You know 'em?" the sheriff asked when Law had finished.

The bounty hunter shook his head. "Never did get the name of two of 'em. They didn't exactly introduce themselves before they started stirrin' up trouble. The other one told me his name was Corwin. Wally Corwin." Judging by the look on McCracken's weather-beaten face, the sheriff had heard of Corwin. "You know him?"

McCracken nodded, but said nothing.

Law was a little surprised when the sheriff remained silent. "I reckon I ain't shocked at that notion," he said. "Considerin' how him and his cronies were actin' out at the Honegger farm, I expect they've had run-ins with the law before. I reckon you'll know the others, too, once you look at 'em."

"Reckon I will," McCracken said.

To Law, the sheriff seemed preoccupied. "Something stuck in your craw, Jess?" he asked, an eyebrow raised in question.

McCracken shook his head, as if trying to clear out the cobwebs of worry. "Naw. Reckon not, J.T." He smiled a bit, looking more like himself. "Well, John Thomas, let's go get these boys over to the undertaker's. After bein' in this heat since yesterday afternoon, they're gonna be gittin' ripe before much longer."

Law nodded. "Lead on, McCracken," he said with a tight grin. Something was bothering his friend; he knew that much. And it irritated him that he didn't know what it was.

McCracken took the ropes to the three body-laden horses, while Law took Toby's reins in hand. "This way," the sheriff said, heading off up the street. As they strolled, Law was aware of the townspeople stopping to stare at the odd little procession. He knew they were wondering about him—and about the corpses. But he could also see their respect for the county sheriff. It was, Law remembered, always that way with people who knew Jesse McCracken. The former Rebel guerrilla, onetime Texas Ranger, and present-day county sheriff was small in statue. Many a man had thought he could take advantage of McCracken's lack of height. And a goodly number of those fools never lived to regret having such wrongheaded notions. Jess McCracken could hold his own with men many times his size. He had shown all his life that he was strong, determined, and devoid of fear. He was also

relentless when he had made up his mind that he was right—
and when someone did something dastardly. As hard a man
as McCracken was, he was not one to allow harm to women and
children. It had brought him into conflict with his Confederate
guerrilla commanders, William Quantrill and Bill Anderson,
more than once.

Law glanced over at the feisty little man, who strutted
rather than walked up the dusty main street. He had changed
some in appearance since the war days—he was stouter, with
a bit of a belly hanging over his gun belt, and his face showed
the wear of time and weather. But he still walked with a swag-
ger, his back remained straight as a rifle barrel, and there was
the same old determination in his crystal blue eyes.

The undertaker's shop—run by the Trigueras brothers, Pedro
and Pablo—was only half a dozen doors up from the sheriff's
office, on the other side of the wide main street. It had a large
glass window with the name in fancy painted lettering next
to the wide wood door with a thin double window in the top
half.

Law and McCracken were tying the horses to the hitching
rail out front when Pedro Trigueras, a tall, thin, nattily attired
man, stepped out of the building, smiling at them. The prospect
of three county-paid-for burials brightened his day.

"Looks like we got some business for you and your brother,
Pedro," McCracken said.

"Plenty business, señor." Trigueras's eyes gleamed.

"We'll bring 'em 'round back," the sheriff said. "Get some
of your boys out there to haul 'em inside. Pronto."

"Sí, Señor Sheriff." Pedro turned and headed back inside
his funeral parlor, moving as elegantly as he was dressed.

With Law leading his horse and McCracken doing the same
with the grisly cargo, they went around the corner of the wood
building, down the alleyway, and around the back corner, stopping at a wide door. Moments later, the door opened and two
husky young Mexican men stepped out. Their plain clothes
were covered by aprons coated with dried blood and other un-
mentionable stains.

With ease, the two lifted each canvas-wrapped corpse from
the horse one at a time and carried it into the building. Law

and McCracken stood nearby, waiting silently, until all three bodies were inside. They tied the horses to a hitching rail and then went inside.

It was dim despite several lanterns, and the place was rank with the smell of death and rotting flesh. Inside the large room were half a dozen plain wood tables, four of them occupied, three of them with the bodies the two lawmen had just delivered.

"Cut that canvas off, boys, so we can get a look at 'em," McCracken ordered.

The two Mexicans quickly sliced through the coverings on the bodies and peeled them away. The stench in the hot room grew considerably by the time they were done.

Trying to ignore the stink, McCracken moved up and looked at the face of each dead man. "Roy Stroud," he said at the first one, then, "Corwin. And this here one is Nelson Rohmer." His voice was harsh.

"I take it you know those two others, too," Law commented.

McCracken nodded. He did not look happy.

"Is there paper out on them?" Law asked. He could see no reason not to pick up some extra money if the men were wanted and had prices on their heads.

"I reckon so," McCracken allowed. He remained staring at the bodies a few moments longer, then spun and bellowed, "Pedro!"

When the elegant Mexican undertaker appeared from the front part of his funeral home, McCracken said, "Best get these boys taken care of right soon, amigo. In this heat, they're already gittin' purty ripe. They don't need nothin' special, as far as I'm concerned. And don't bother sendin' the bill to the county. Send it to that bastard Chester Kuykendall. You might want to have someone talk to him first, though. While I doubt it, he might want these boys' funeral fancied up some."

"*Sí,* señor," Trigueras said evenly.

McCracken gave a curt nod, then headed for the back door. "Come on, J.T.," he said as he moved.

Law followed the sheriff outside. "Who's this Kuykendall?" he asked.

"We'll talk about it later," McCracken said gruffly. He untied the dead men's horses and mounted one of them. "We'd best get your horse over to the livery, J.T.," he noted. "Then I expect you could do with some grub."

"I do have a mite of an appetite," Law allowed. He was a tad annoyed at his old friend. Something was going on here, and he was not privy to it, which irked him. Making it worse was the fact that McCracken was unwilling to talk about it. He had half a mind to just ride on out of town, but that would be downright foolish. At least without listening to what McCracken would have to say to him. After all, the sheriff had wired him to come here for some reason.

Besides, there was no other place nearby, and Law was in the mood for a real bed for a change for at least a few days, some halfway decent whiskey, some good food and, for certain, a woman. So he would try to keep his temper in check while he bided his time. He did vow to himself, however, that if McCracken wasn't forthcoming with some information soon, he was going to take his pleasure here and then ride out. Let his old friend find someone else to do whatever nasty or difficult task he wanted Law to do. And the bounty hunter knew it had to be something nasty or difficult—or perhaps even somewhat illegal—or else he would have taken care of it himself.

Law pulled himself into the saddle on Toby. "Lead on, McCracken," he said. The joke was already old, even to him.

O'Fallon's Livery was on Third Street, which ran at right angles to Main Street, at the end of Douglas Street. It consisted of a massive barn and a large, sprawling corral. Owner Sean O'Fallon was a tall, whiskey-smelling, blustery, florid-faced man in his fifties with a mop of stringy reddish hair hanging down from the back of his battered cloth cap. He talked with McCracken for a few moments, then led the dead men's horses away toward the barn.

Law took his Winchester rifle and saddlebags off of Toby and turned the horse over to O'Fallon when the livery man returned.

"This's some animal, boy-o," O'Fallon said as he took Toby's reins. "You ever think of sellin' him? I'd give you top dollar for him."

Law looked at the man as if he had lost all reason.

"Well, I reckon not, then, eh?" O'Fallon muttered as he led the horse away.

"You just best treat him well, boy," Law warned. The statement was greeted by a vague wave of the hand.

"The horse'll be all right, J.T.," McCracken said. "O'Fallon's a man who has a mighty big likin' for bug juice, but he knows horses. And more important, he likes 'em."

"Good thing. He hurts Toby, he'll be the Trigueras brothers' next customer."

McCracken said nothing as he and Law walked back to Main Street. After getting Law a room at the Llano House—a second story room that offered a vague view of the distant clump of trees that surrounded the spring that had given the town its name—the two went next door to the attached restaurant. Both ate heartily of beefsteak, fried-up potatoes, and beans, washed down with fresh milk, then followed by cherry cobbler and coffee. The men ate in silence, more interested in filling their stomachs than in conversation.

Finally, though, Law pulled out a thin cigar and fired it up. Relaxing back in his chair with the cigar in one hand and coffee mug in the other, he asked, "So, tell me, Jess, how'd you come to be a county sheriff?"

"You remember I came back home to Texas that time during the war when I was shot up so bad in that fracas up there in Kansas?" When Law nodded, he continued. "Well, by the time I was ready for fightin' again, the war was over."

From that point, he had taken a different path than Law had. Where Law had, because of personal reasons, briefly joined the James and Younger boys in some of their outlawry, Jesse McCracken had joined the Texas Rangers when he found that trying to farm his family's plot of land was too troublesome with the contentious Yankee government in charge, and the even more odious carpetbaggers running whatever else the army or government officials weren't.

After almost a decade of running around Texas chasing Comanches, outlaws, and Mexican bandits, McCracken had decided it was time to settle down. It helped that he met Lucy Mae Willoughby right about that time. Lucy Mae was a head taller than Jess McCracken, and she was willowy and red-haired. He fell for her the moment he set eyes on her. Luckily for him, she felt the same. They married, and he tried settling down again, once more trying to make a go of a small farm outside of the recently established town of Big Spring. But it seemed that whatever farming blood he might have once had was long gone.

He was struggling with it when town and county officials approached him after a bank robbery in the fast-growing town. In the ensuing gunbattle, the county sheriff and a deputy had been killed. The town marshal said chasing after the outlaws was not his job once they had left the town limits. So the officials had come to McCracken and asked him to chase the men down. After all, they told him, he had experience in the Late Unpleasantness as well as being a Texas Ranger. There was no one more qualified than he to chase these men down.

So he had been appointed interim Howard County sheriff, raised a posse, and went after the robbers. When McCracken and his men had brought the robbers to justice, the town fathers and county officials were so grateful that they gave McCracken the sheriff's post permanently—at least until the next election. McCracken was now in his first full term as Howard County sheriff, and was well respected by most folks in the county and beyond.

"And, you know, J.T., I really do like it," McCracken finished with a shrug and an embarrassed chuckle. He paused, then asked, "Whatever happened to that gal you was sweet on? What was her name? Sara?"

"Sara Jane Woodall," Law said flatly. He hesitated to say more, then decided there was no reason not to tell it. "Like you, I had trouble with the damned Yankees. They made it damned hard on us, and after the folks died, the farm was sold off for taxes. And, with the feud between my folks and Sara Jane's still boiling over, she cast me over. Wasn't much for me to do at that point but leave the state and seek my fortunes elsewhere." He glanced askance at McCracken as he took a sip of coffee.

"Ridin' with outlaws was no way to make your fortune, J.T.," McCracken said quietly.

Law looked sharply at him. "You know?"

McCracken nodded.

"Well, that didn't set well with me neither, so's I left Missouri and skedaddled back to Texas. But with paper out on me up in Missouri and Kansas, and few prospects at home, Sara Jane still wouldn't have wanted no part of me, even if I could've found her."

"That when you took to overindulgin' in rotgut?" There was no condescension in his voice.

Law nodded. "But a few years of that was more than enough for this fella. Soon after, I took to bounty huntin'." He paused to finish his mug of coffee, which he put back on the table. "Which brings me to why I'm here." He stared at McCracken. "Why *am* I here, Jess?"

CHAPTER 4

✦

"I THINK I need me a snort or two while I'm fillin' you in, J.T.," McCracken said, rising.

Law followed suit, and they headed out. McCracken led the way across the street to a saloon called the Wellspring. It was one of the better places in town, with a real mahogany bar forming an open square in the center of the saloon. It was surrounded by regular tables and a variety of gambling tables. Most of the latter were in use. Cyprians worked the room, clad in scanty but fairly expensive garments. When they weren't pushing drinks, they were taking men upstairs to the bedrooms on the second floor for business.

McCracken pointed and said, "There's an empty table over in that corner, J.T. Go and grab it while I get us somethin' to wet our whistles."

"Just make sure it ain't rotgut," Law responded as he headed for the table.

Moments later McCracken joined him, placing a bottle of whiskey, two glasses, and two big cigars on the table. He sat as Law pulled the cork on the bottle and poured them each a drink. Each took a sip of the whiskey. Law pronounced it good enough and then picked up one of the cigars. He lit it, and McCracken did the same with the other.

"You remember that fella Chester Kuykendall I mentioned before?" McCracken finally asked.

Law nodded.

"The damn Yankee owns a ranch a couple of miles southwest of town. It's gettin' to be a mighty big spread, too. Runs a couple hundred head of cattle. Horses, too. But he's really buildin' his wealth and power by deviltry—cattle and horse rustling mostly, and bank and stage robberies. Of course, there's always the rape and murder that such miscreants favor."

"Sounds like a right busy fella," Law allowed, blowing a smoke ring toward the ceiling.

"Well, he's too damn smart to actually be present during most of these misdeeds. For the most part, he plans these things, then sends his small army out to do his biddin'. Of course, he takes most of the loot."

"Of course," Law said dryly. He had seen it so many times. Indeed, he had encountered such men far more often than he cared to remember—and had collected rewards on most of those.

"Every once in a while, though, that son of a bitch likes to take part in some of the devilish deeds."

"So what's the problem? Why don't you just round him and his cronies up, try 'em all, and ship 'em off to the nearest prison? Or hang 'em."

"It ain't that easy, John Thomas," McCracken said with a sigh. "People hereabouts want civilization, so we're tryin' to do it legal, but we ain't had much luck at it so far."

"You want me to take care of this bunch, is that it, Jess?" Law asked. It was becoming clear to him. It was what he did, and it seemed only reasonable that McCracken, if he was having trouble putting an end to these cutthroats legally, would want the extralegal services of a bounty man.

"Well, not really," McCracken said. He was having trouble explaining himself, and that soured his humor. He poured them each another drink and took a sip. "Kuykendall must have twenty or thirty men out there—all hard cases and gunmen—as well as at least that many cow punchers, who can, and likely would, use their guns for him, if asked. Sending one man out there—even one as good as you are at these things, J.T.—would be dangerous. Hell, it'd be downright foolish. And I ain't about to ask a friend of mine to go up against such odds."

"I'm obliged," Law said not too sarcastically. John Thomas Law was a fearless man, and one who even had a powerful streak of rashness in him when it was called for. But he did not relish the thought of going against so many guns all by himself.

McCracken offered a wry smile. "Besides, you couldn't get them all at once, and with his resources, Kuykendall would just replace them. And probably damn near as fast as you could take 'em out." He paused to finish off his shot of whiskey and pour another. Then he puffed his cigar for a few moments, gathering his thoughts.

Law did the same, letting his friend take his time. He was comfortable sitting here with a good cigar and some fine whiskey. Especially after the long ride. He was content to sit awhile. He did take the time to scan the room, though, keeping an eye out for any potential troublemakers—though he spotted none—and for any women who might catch his fancy. He was overdue for a roll in the hay—well, actually, a bed—with some lusty female. He saw several likely possibilities.

"We've arrested a number of his men from time to time on a passel of charges," McCracken suddenly continued. "We had us some damned good witnesses all ready to testify, too. Trouble is, when the judge arrived and the time for the trial came, the witnesses never showed up. We found them some time later—dead. Hanged, to be exact. Each had a warnin' pinned to his shirt. Since then, we've had trouble findin' anyone willin' to testify against any of Kuykendall's men."

"Do tell," Law said without surprise.

McCracken grunted by way of response. "So, of course, the judge had to let them go. And out of the courtroom they'd sashay, sneerin' at us the whole time." Anger started to touch his voice. He took his job too seriously to not be enraged at the effrontery of such men leering at his judicial impotence like that.

Law could see the pain of failure on his friend's face and understood it very well. He would feel the same as McCracken if he were in the sheriff's position.

"So, what we need to do," McCracken said in a tight voice, "is to get Kuykendall himself."

"Cut off the head, and the snake will die," Law commented.

"Exactly. If we can do that, it'd go a long way to endin' the heap of crime we've been havin' in Howard County."

"And that's nigh onto impossible because he rarely takes part in any of the crimes," Law guessed.

"That's right," McCracken said sourly. Then he brightened a bit. "But I did say that he took part in some evildoin' from time to time."

Law shot a questioning glance at McCracken through a small cloud of cigar smoke. "And you got him this time, didn't you?"

"Yep," the sheriff said with a tight grin. Then the smile fell. "But therein lies the problem—and why I asked you to come here, J.T."

"How can I help?" This made no sense. He could understand it if perhaps McCracken wanted him to run down Kuykendall's horde of banditti, but he could not fathom what the sheriff would want him to do.

"Well, like I said, because of all those instances of witnesses turnin' up hanged, folks round here've been mighty reluctant to testify against Kuykendall's men, let alone Kuykendall himself."

Judging by McCracken's taut jaw and determined eyes, Law knew there was a "but" coming.

"But," the sheriff continued, "we've got one fella who's willin' to testify against Kuykendall, but he's scared."

"So?" Law wasn't sure he liked where this was heading.

"So, what I need for you to do is protect this fella till the judge arrives."

"You want me to nursemaid some fella till the trial?" Law asked.

"Yep. It's less than two weeks. Once he testifies, Kuykendall'll be done for. He'll be hanged sure as hell, and then we can go back to livin' peaceful around here."

"What've you been doin' with him till now?"

"Keepin' him under wraps, and sweatin' bullets. I can't keep him hidden forever, and I can't watch over him all the time. Me and my deputies are havin' a devil of a time just tryin' to keep Kuykendall's men from breaking Kuykendall out of jail—or from having townspeople break in and lynch the bastard. I'd just go and let the people have him, but that goes against the grain for me."

McCracken paused, downing another shot. He picked up the bottle to refill his glass, then set it down again. He had had enough. "You done with this, J.T.?" he asked.

Law nodded, and McCracken stuck the cork back in the bottle.

"Anyways, John Thomas, I was just waitin' for you to get here. You're the only one I can trust with somethin' like this."

"I'd like to help you, Jess, I surely would," Law said with some regret in his voice, "but I'm a bounty man, not a bodyguard." He rolled the empty whiskey glass around in his hands, though he kept his eyes on McCracken's.

"I know that, J.T. But from what I know about you from our days with the guerrillas—and from what I've heard about you over the past several years—I have a lot of faith that you can handle this. Hell, boy, your reputation alone'll give most of Kuykendall's men pause should they be considerin' goin' against you. Ain't nobody else I know would be able to pull that off."

"What about the Rangers?" Law asked. "You should have some friends among 'em from the days you rode with 'em."

"I do," McCracken said with a nod. "But they got their hands full with troublemakers all across the state. Plus there's still some Comanch' renegades stirrin' up trouble now and again. And beyond that, a heap of damned Mexican bandidos keep comin' across the border to stir up some deviltry." He sighed as he contemplated the smoke drifting up from his cigar. "I tried tellin' them boys that sooner or later, Kuykendall is gonna spread out from Howard County. It ain't gonna be long if he manages to somehow go free after this trial."

"And they still wouldn't offer any help?" Law asked. He was already beginning to consider wiring his old friend Abe Covington, a captain who commanded a troop of Texas Rangers from a base in Austin, for some help for McCracken. Covington would know McCracken, as the Ranger had also ridden with Law and McCracken during the war.

"I think most of the Rangers know that," the sheriff responded. "At least the ones in the field and the ones who run things around these parts, But the high-up muckety-mucks back in Austin . . ." He saw the sudden darkening of Law's face and half-smiled. "No, Abe ain't one of the ones I'm talkin' about," he added. "In fact, I wired him hinting that I could use some Ranger help, but he messaged back that there wasn't nothin' he could do."

Law nodded. If Covington had said he couldn't help, it would be the truth. He would never turn down helping a friend—especially an old comrade-in-arms and onetime fellow Ranger—unless there was a powerful reason not to. Law suspected that Covington was involved in some operation about now.

"What about the town marshal?" Law asked. "Can't you get any help from him?"

"Fred Langenfeld?" McCracken said with a snort of derision. "He's about as useful as tits on a bull." His voice harshened. "I can't prove it, but I'd swear on my dear departed mother's grave that that son of a bitch is on Kuykendall's payroll. He won't do squat about Kuykendall. Claims that if Kuykendall was involved in any crimes, they were done for the most part outside of Big Spring, so they're out of his jurisdiction."

"Ain't this witness of yours a townsman?"

"No. But even if he was, it wouldn't mean a damn thing for that piss-poor excuse of a marshal. He just keeps sayin' it's my problem, and he can't spare any deputies to help out, since it's not really town business."

Law ground his teeth. He hated such men, ones who used their position for their own gain without regard to what they were supposed to do or what was, by law, required of them. He had not long ago run into a lawman who, like this Langenfeld appeared to be, was on the payroll of a big-time outlaw. That law dog had gotten in over his head and had paid for it

with his life—killed by men sent by the man whose payroll he
was on. He figured that this Langenfeld would suffer the same
fate—unless he first angered McCracken to the point where
the sheriff took care of it.

Still, it did not really change Law's mind about taking the
job. On the other hand, he did not like turning down a friend
who was asking for help.

McCracken could see the quandary writ large on Law's
face. "I really need your help, J.T.," he said earnestly. "I got
no one else I can turn to—and no one else I can trust with
such a job." He was ashamed at having to plead for help, but
he was a big enough man inside that he had no compunction
about doing so, because this job needed doing.

Law felt himself weakening a bit. It was mighty difficult
for him to sit here and see his friend's shame at asking him for
help.

"Look, J.T.," the sheriff said, leaning forward until his
forearms were resting on the table, "I understand you don't do
much for nothing. At least where it concerns your business. If
that's the case, I'm prepared to offer you five hundred dollars
to accept."

Law's ears perked up, and he began to see an end to his
quandary.

"And that'll be in addition to any rewards that are out for
any of Kuykendall's men you might bring in." Law's immediate future was clearing up rapidly.

"Like I said, I expect there's rewards out for them three
sidewinders you brung into town with you. I don't think
they'll be worth more than a few bucks, but that'd be a little
extra in your pocket." He suddenly began to get angry at the
idea of having to bribe an old comrade to do something to
help him, though when he thought about it for a moment, he
realized that it wasn't really a bribe. After all, he couldn't expect a man to ride all this way and put his life on the line for
no remuneration. Friendship wasn't that strong, not unless it
involved family or something.

"Plus," McCracken pressed on, "all your expenses'll be
paid for by the county—room, grub, horse care, whatever supplies you need."

Law suddenly grinned. "That include a woman, should there be a need to pay for one for some sportin'?" he asked.

McCracken laughed and relaxed a little. "I'd be hard-pressed to explain that to county officials," he said. "But I reckon I could manage to slip it by 'em, should the need for it arise."

McCracken paused, watching Law intently. After some moments, he asked, "So, John Thomas, are you in or not?"

CHAPTER 5

"ALL RIGHT, JESS," Law said. "I'll do it. I can't make any guarantees, though. Like I said, this ain't my usual line of work."

Relief washed across McCracken's face. "You'll do just fine, pard," he said. He leaned back, relatively relaxed, and puffed on his fat cigar.

"So, tell me about this Kuykendall," Law urged. He reached out, pulled the cork from the bottle, and poured himself another snort. He waggled the bottle at McCracken, but the sheriff shook his head. Law stoppered the bottle again, then took a sip of whiskey.

"Don't know too much of his background. Like I told you, he's a damn Yankee," he said with distaste. "Damned carpetbagger. Don't know what he did durin' the war, but we heard tell he was some kind of cavalry officer. I ain't sure when he come to Texas, but he got here a few years ago and took over a small ranch used to belong to one of us." He grimaced at the remembrance.

"Meanin' a true Texan," Law noted.

"Yep," the sheriff said with a nod. "A longtime Texan who wrested this land from the hands of the heathen Comanch' and whose blood has stained the ground. Then this cussed mudsill comes along and downright steals it from him. Drove that poor family off to God knows where." His anger was stirring again.

"Maybe I will have another shot of that there red-eye," McCracken muttered, filling his small glass and downing it in one quick jolt.

"A lot of Texans've been though such a thing, Jess," Law commented quietly.

"I know," McCracken responded. "But it still galls me, J.T."

Law nodded in understanding.

"As far as I know, he started hirin' guns—and raisin' hell—soon after he got that land. He and I have been lockin' horns since I become sheriff."

"Was he involved in the ruckus that got you hired in the first place?" Law asked.

McCracken shrugged. "I reckon so, but I didn't know anything about Kuykendall at the time, and I can't prove it now. But after all I've learned, it seems unlikely anyone else would have robbed a bank that way and caused so much trouble in this county without Kuykendall's approval—or at least knowledge." He tugged at his full, shaggy mustache with a couple of fingers. "If I'd known when I was chasin' those galoots what I know about Kuykendall now, I would've—"

"Well, you didn't know," Law said flatly. "So there's not a damn thing you could've done about it then, and you're tryin' to do somethin' about it now."

"Yeah. I reckon."

"So where is this ranch?"

"The Double Bar K is five, six miles southwest of Big Spring. Kuykendall has a large ranch house where he lives with his wife, Lorita, a half-Mexican, half-Choctaw with a well-rounded figure and a smile that I'm told devastates men. Now I ain't given to speakin' ill of women, but from everything I've ever heard, that there woman is one evil she-wolf. I wouldn't even be surprised if she took part in some of the ventures her husband concocts."

Law was surprised at the vehemence in McCracken's voice. His description of this woman was pretty strong by Mc-Cracken's standards.

McCracken sighed, putting a lid on his anger. "And, like I said earlier, he has twenty, thirty guns at any one time. There are two bunkhouses on the ranch, where they stay between 'jobs.' Plus another one for his regular cowhands. There's also a huge barn, large enough for most of the men's horses, though many of the horses are usually out on the prairie so they can forage."

Law nodded, tiring of it all in some ways. As it was, if he did what he was being hired to do, he would not really have anything to do with Chester Kuykendall or his hellacious wife or the army of gunmen the rancher had at his command. Of course, it was quite likely that he would face some of those hard cases, since it seemed probable that Kuykendall already knew about the man who was going to testify against him. And if he didn't, Kuykendall would assuredly hear about him soon and would undoubtedly send some of his men to find—and kill—him. And that, of course, is what Law had been hired to prevent.

"Well, Jess," Law finally said, "I reckon you've got a passel of things to attend to. Why don't you go on about your business." He offered the barest hint of a smile. "And I'll go about mine for now."

McCracken grinned. "I bet you will." Then he grew serious. "But first, don't you want to know about the witness? His name's Hank Blackstone, by the way."

"I reckon that can wait till mornin', Jess. Besides, I don't figure there's too much I really need to know about him before I take on lookin' after him. Most of what I do need to know, I can learn from him since we'll be spendin' all our time together, me and him."

McCracken nodded and rose. "Keep the bottle," he said, then wondered if maybe that was not too much temptation for a man who had for some years had trouble with red-eye. But then he decided that was foolish. John Thomas Law had not forged the reputation he had by still being overly tempted by the bottle. "I'll see you at my office first thing in the mornin'. You all right on cash?"

"I'm fine."

Jamming the half-smoked cigar in his mouth under the flapping mustache, McCracken turned and strutted out the door, a banty rooster with no fear in him.

Law grinned as he watched the sheriff for a moment. Then he grabbed the bottle and poured himself a drink. He sipped it, waiting, as his eyes scanned the room, finally settling on a pert redhead of medium height and bodacious figure.

She caught his glance and, with a smile, sashayed over to the table where Law sat. She perched on his lap and wrapped her arms around his neck. "Lonely, cowpoke?" she asked in a lust-drenched voice.

"I am," Law responded, caught up in the sheen of sweat that glistened on her soft, white shoulders and ample cleavage. "But I ain't no cowpoke."

"Sorry, sweetheart," she whispered. "I shoulda known by these duds you're wearin'." She pulled one hand from around his neck and ran it along the edge of his frock coat's lapel. "Much too fine for some cow puncher."

"You up for a fandango tonight?" Law asked.

"Whoo-eee," the woman said, eyelashes fluttering. "You think mighty high of yourself to think you can play all night, mister."

He grinned. "Any man ain't sure of himself in such matters ain't much of a man a'tall," he allowed. "What's your name, darlin'?"

"Jessamine."

"Purty name." He grasped her around the waist and lifted her up and off of him. Then he reached into a pocket inside his coat and pulled out a small wad of greenbacks. He counted some off and held it out to her. As she went to take it, he grabbed her hand. "You will be back after you pay your boss," he said, not asked.

A bit of fear flickered across her face but quickly passed. She saw danger in his eyes but also decency. Even if she wasn't certain that he would hurt her if she stiffed him, she was too interested in this tall, hard man to want to. She smiled. "You bet, Mr. . . . ?"

"You can call me J.T."

"I'll be back directly, Mr. . . . J.T." She hurried off.

Law watched her, not because he thought she was lying to him, but because he liked the way her hips swung as she walked. It was a mighty tasty sight. He was still watching as she headed back to him after handing the bartender the money and talking with him a moment. Law thought the sight from the front was even better.

He rose as she neared the table. With the bottle in one hand, the other around Jessamine, and the cigar firmly planted in his mouth, Law headed outside and led Jessamine to his room in the Llano House. There he stubbed the cigar out and poured them each a drink in two of the four glasses that had been resting on the bureau against one wall. When they were done with the drink, Law reached out, grabbed Jessamine, pulled her to him gently, then kissed her hard.

Minutes later, they were naked and moaning on the big, comfortable bed.

AFTER A FINAL roll in the blankets, Law sent Jessamine on her way the next morning with an extra ten dollars. "Now that's for you," he said to her as he sent her out the door with a swat on her behind. "You ain't to fork over none of it to that no-'count crook you work for, you understand?"

She stopped just outside the door and looked back. She nodded and gave him a radiant smile before leaving.

Law went back inside and cleaned himself up as best he could. He considered taking a bath but decided against it for two reasons: he didn't really have the time, and since he could already tell, even though the sun had barely risen, that it was going to be another scorcher of a day, it would do little good.

He did, however, put on a fresh shirt before leaving the room. He stood outside the Llano House for a few moments, watching the townspeople go about their business. Then he stepped off the veranda and went next door, where he filled up on a good breakfast of hen's eggs, flapjacks, and coffee. Finished, he headed across Main Street to Wentworth's Dry Goods.

It was dim inside the store, and several degrees cooler than outside. Law walked toward the back, where a counter ran crossways most of the width of the store. An older man and a boy of about ten years old waited on two hard-looking men. Seeing Law, the older man broke away and came to where Law waited at the counter.

"May I help you, mister?" the man asked. Below his mostly bald pate, his pasty face wore a sheen of sweat and worry, and sunken eyes kept flicking back toward the two other customers and the boy.

"I'll take me a dozen of them slim cigars there," Law said, pointing to the ones he wanted in a glass case on the counter.

The man pulled them out and, with a shaky hand, set them on the counter. "That'll be—" A resounding slap stopped him, and he jerked his head around. What little color he had in his face drained away.

Law, too, looked down the counter. The boy was holding a hand to his face, which was already showing some discoloration, and a trickle of blood seeped from the corner of the boy's mouth.

"I told you I wanted Arbuckle's coffee, boy," one of the hard cases snapped. "Not that there crap you're tryin' to foist off on us."

"But I . . ." the boy started, sounding near tears, then tried again. "You never said Arbuckle's. Just coffee, mister. I—"

"Don't you sass me, you little peckerwood," the man snarled. He backhanded the boy across the other side of his face.

Looking like he was going to piddle in his trousers, the old man took a step in that direction, but Law reached out and grabbed him by the arm. "Just stay put, friend," he said quietly. He turned and headed toward the two men and the boy. The man who had hit the boy twice was rearing back for another blow.

"That would be a damfool thing to do," Law said. Though he had not raised his voice, he could be heard perfectly well. He stopped about three feet from the two men.

Both turned to face him, the one dropping his arm. The hitter had a permanent scowl on his face, which was marked by a thick scar that ran from the outside corner of the left eyebrow down his cheek and ended just on the underside of the chin. He was almost as tall as Law but thin and wiry. His eyes seemed dead. The other was a man who gave ugliness a bad name: a gray lump of a face that was heavily pockmarked with pieces of skin peeling away and dotted with moles. He was about five foot nine but weighed at least two hundred and fifty pounds, most of it flab. Both hadn't shaved in days and hadn't bathed in weeks, perhaps months.

"This ain't none of your affair, mister," Scar Face said.

"I usually make it my business when some walkin' piece of buffalo shit starts whompin' on youngsters."

"I'm warnin' you, boy," Scar Face growled, "to go about your business and keep your nose out of this."

"A warnin'?" Law chuckled, but there was no humor in it. "A warnin' from the likes of you ain't worth spit, bub," Law allowed. "Now I suggest you and your scabrous pardner let this young fella tote up what you owe, then pay him and get your festerin' asses out of here."

"You believe this asshole, Clem?" Scar Face said over his shoulder to his companion.

"Boy's got some stones on 'em, I reckon, Billy," Clem responded. "Cain't say he's got much in the way of smarts, though."

"That's a fact, Clem." Billy had not taken his eyes off Law during the short exchange. "Look, mister, I don't know who the hell you are, but—"

"Name's Law. John Thomas Law."

Billy's eyes widened a bit at the news, but he was not about to let the fact that he was facing bounty hunter J.T. Law make him back down. He had heard of Law, but he was not worried about stories. Most turned out to be exaggerated anyway. "Well, now, I really don't give a goddamn hoot who you are. But you're messin' in business ain't none of your concern. Now, you seem to be new to these parts, and, me bein' the decent feller I am, I'm gonna let this transgression pass. But only if you just march yourself out of here right now."

He paused to let that sink in, becoming somewhat surprised when it had no effect at all on the big, broad-shouldered man facing him. He began to wonder if there weren't more to the stories about J.T. Law than he had thought.

"I got a better idea, boys," Law said in quiet but powerful tones. "You do what I already said, and you'll walk out of here alive."

Clem laughed. "What a dunce."

His and Billy's faces grew hard, and both men went for their pistols at the same time.

CHAPTER 6

✶

LAW TOOK A step forward. With his left hand he grabbed Billy's gun arm, holding it fast so the man could not pull his pistol. Law yanked out his Peacemaker and cracked Billy across the head with the barrel. As Billy slumped to the floor, dazed but not quite out, Law moved back a step or two to get out of the way and slid back the hammer of the Colt.

Clem still had not cleared leather. "Don't do it, bub," Law warned, voice controlled and certain.

"Go to hell, bounty man," Clem snarled, finally managing to get his pistol out of the holster. As he began bringing it to bear on Law, the bounty hunter fired twice.

The two bullets—one to the forehead, the other to the chest—punched Clem back a few steps, and then he fell with a flatulent sigh, dead before he settled on the dusty wood floor.

Law shook his head in annoyance as he noticed that the woozy Billy was still trying to get his revolver out. Law squatted and stuck the muzzle of his Peacemaker gently in the center of Billy's forehead. "You really don't want to pull that piece, bub," he warned.

Billy's eyes were suddenly wide with fear. He had seriously underestimated this man, and he was sure now that he was going to die, though he had to try to live. "No, I don't," he said, shaking his head as best he could with the gun barrel resting right there on his forehead.

"Smart move, pard." Law reached out with his left hand, groping for a second until he encountered the man's pistol. He pulled it free. He glanced to make sure it was not cocked, then looked over at the old man who was standing there, his hands on the boy's shoulders. Both looked scared to death. Law tossed the pistol toward them, and the boy awkwardly caught it.

Law rose. Though the Peacemaker came away from Billy's skin, it did not waver from being aimed at the same spot on his head. "Up," he commanded. When Billy was on his feet, Law relieved him of the large knife he had in a sheath on the opposite side of his gun belt from the holster. He handed that to the old man.

"Keep those for the time bein'," Law said. "I'll see that someone gets down here directly to get Clem out of here."

The old man nodded, still looking frightened, but having calmed down a little.

"All right, Mr. Billy," Law said, "let's go pay us a visit to the marshal."

At gunpoint, Law marched Billy up Main Street to Marshal Fred Langenfeld's office, drawing a sizable crowd of onlookers along the way.

Inside, Marshal Langenfeld's face went white when he saw Billy and Law. The bounty hunter thought that was strange, but he let it pass.

"What's this, Billy?" Langenfeld demanded, regaining some of his equilibrium. He pushed himself up from his seat behind the desk, resting his palms on the top.

"You know this man, Marshal?" Law interjected.

"Billy Crawford?" He leaned forward on his hands a little. "Yes, I know him. What's he done?"

"Him and another blockhead—ugliest goddamn fella I ever saw—"

"Clem Dillman," Langenfeld said.

Law shrugged. "As I was startin' to say, the two knotheads

was manhandlin' some boy workin' over at Wentworth's store. When I suggested that such behavior was unbecomin' in two grown men, they disagreed and set out to draw down on me."

"That's a goddamn lie," Crawford snapped. "You know me and Clem better than that, Marshal. We wouldn't go pullin' guns on some feller. Sure, I cuffed that kid upside the head, but it wasn't hard, and, hell, that dumb little bastard deserved it."

While listening to Crawford, Law watched Langenfeld's face. It went from confusion to worry to anger to disgust. It was interesting, and Law wondered what it all meant. He did remember that McCracken had said it seemed likely that Langenfeld was in the pocket of Chester Kuykendall, which would explain some of the emotions he had just seen played out across the marshal's face. But it would not explain some others.

"So you and Clem was just pure innocent, were you?" Langenfeld demanded.

"Damn right. We was mindin' our own business, buyin' some supplies, and aimin' to teach that little brat some manners, when this peckerwood stuck his nose in—"

Law whacked Crawford on the side of the head with the barrel of the Peacemaker, though not as hard as last time. It staggered him again but didn't knock him down.

"Shut your big bazoo, bub," Law said not unharshly. "Even a scrofulous cockroach like you should know it ain't right to tell lies. Especially such whoppers."

Langenfeld glared at Crawford for a bit, a range of emotions still crisscrossing his face. He was in a bind here and didn't know quite how to get out of it.

Holding his bleeding head, Crawford growled, "You gonna let this asshole get away with hittin' me right in front of you like this, Marshal? And get away with killin' Clem?"

"You killed Dillman?" Langenfeld asked, eyes shooting to Law.

"Yep," the bounty man responded without hesitation. "I gave the damfool a chance to walk out, but he insisted on pullin' his piece on me. So I showed him the error of his ways. Had he left that hogleg where it was, he'd still be alive and me and this stupid son of a bitch wouldn't be standin' here."

"You gonna listen to this bullshit, Marshal?" Crawford asked, voice hard.

Before the lawman could respond—he was taking his time thinking over a response—Law slid the Peacemaker into the strapped-down holster. Then he grabbed Crawford by the back of the shirt and shoved him forward a couple of steps, smashing the man's face against the wall. Jerking him backward and around by the collar of his shirt, Law mostly held Crawford up in front of Langenfeld's desk, behind which the marshal still stood, watching.

"I don't know what kind of hold you got or think you got on the marshal here, bub," Law said harshly, "but if you open your mouth one more goddamn time, you'll join your friend Clem in the boneyard." He turned a harsh stare on Langenfeld. "And I don't know what hold this man has on you, Marshal, but I ain't about to stand here and listen to such bushwa said about me. This goddamn skunk and his ugly-as-sin pardner were manhandlin' a boy couldn't be more than ten years old. When I suggested they stop, both went for their pistols. One of 'em's dead, and this one here"—he shook Crawford a little—"would've been, too, had it not been for my good nature. Now, lock this peckerwood up and send somebody down to Wentworth's to drag that scurrilous bastard Dillman out of there."

"I don't know who you are," Langenfeld barked. "But I do not take kindly to bein' given orders in my office in my town, boy."

Law shrugged. "Don't much make me no nevermind what you take kindly to or not, Marshal," he said flatly. "I just expect you to do your damn job."

"Just who the hell are you, anyway?" Langenfeld demanded.

Billy Crawford grinned through the blood on his face in anticipation. Langenfeld, of course, saw it, and wondered what it meant.

"John Thomas Law."

Langenfeld blanched. "What're you doin' in Big Spring?" he asked when he got over the shock of the news.

"Come to visit an old friend," Law said easily.

"And who would that be?"

"Not that it's any of your concern, but it's Sheriff Mc-Cracken."

Langenfeld's eyes widened as he was surprised again. What would a bounty man be doing here visiting the county sheriff? he wondered.

Before Langenfeld could ask any more questions, Law said, "I reckon there's reward money on both these skunks. I expect to collect it. Soon."

Langenfeld nodded, looking rather sick. "All right, Billy," he finally said, "let's go. You know where the cells are."

"I ain't—"

The marshal glared at him, and Crawford clapped his mouth shut. He shuffled forward, the pain in his face and head starting to register. That made it hard to think, but he would have to do something about his treatment not only at Langenfeld's hands but also at Law's.

As Law stepped out into the street, he reached for a cigar in an inner coat pocket. He realized he had only one there and remembered that he had not picked up the ones he was in the process of buying at Wentworth's when the trouble with Crawford and Dillman began. He would have to get back there soon, but now he had better get over to McCracken's. He had been delayed far long enough.

He stepped off the wood sidewalk and strolled across the street, avoiding wagons, horses, and dogs. The county sheriff's office was across Main Street and two doors down from the marshal's.

McCracken was waiting for him, sitting behind his battered wood desk and looking nervous. He rose as Law entered. "Where the hell've you been, J.T.?" he asked.

"I went to Wentworth's to get some cigars and had a run-in with a couple of pukes who were whompin' on some youngster."

"Who were they?"

"Marshal Langenfeld said their names were—"

"Fred got involved?" McCracken asked, surprised.

Law shrugged as he went to the coffeepot and poured himself a tin mug full. He sat at a chair near the corner of McCracken's desk. "Both of 'em tried to draw down on me. I sent one of 'em to meet his maker. The other had enough sense to cease resistin', so I hauled him over to the marshal's."

"You said Fred told you their names?"

"Clem Dillman—he's the one ready for the boneyard—and Billy Crawford."

"Damn," McCracken spat out.

It suddenly hit Law. "More of Kuykendall's men?" he asked.

"Yep."

Law shrugged. "To hell with them. All this means is that there's two less of 'em to be concerned about."

"Fred's not gonna keep Billy in jail more than a couple of hours," McCracken warned.

Law shrugged again. "Still one less to deal with, and Crawford's stove up a little, so he'll be mostly out of action for a couple of days at least."

"I suppose you're right," McCracken said with a sigh that set his mustache flapping. There was silence for a couple of minutes before the sheriff relaxed some. He leaned back, his well-oiled chair not making a sound.

"Where is this Kuykendall anyway?" Law asked.

McCracken jerked his head toward the rear. "Cell in back. There's four cells behind that wall there. No one else is there now. We move him every day from one cell to another, just in case someone tries to break him out from out back."

"Can that be done?"

"It'd be tough. The outside walls are adobe with plankin' over 'em, so they're pretty sturdy. With a concerted effort, it could be done, but by the time they broke through, we'd have Kuykendall out of the cell, and we'd be ready to gun down anyone who managed to get through."

Law nodded. "Can he hear us talkin' out here?"

"Nah. Not if we talk normal. The wall's fairly thick and made of good solid wood."

Law drank coffee for a minute, puffing on his cigar between sips. Then he finally asked, "So where's this Blackstone fella?"

"Small farm outside of town," McCracken said quietly. "He's been there three days."

"You sent him to hide at some farmhouse?" Law was a little incredulous.

"What was I supposed to do with him?" McCracken countered with a little heat. "Put him up in a room at the Llano House? Damn, J.T., you can be exasperatin' at times."

"Don't get your britches on fire, Jess," Law said with a chuckle. "I just meant that it seems odd you'd trust some poor farm folk to watch over him till either I got here and took the job for you or you come up with somethin' else to do if I hadn't been able to show up."

"Not much else I could do. I had him in town here for a couple of days, but keepin' him here any longer was too dangerous.

Law could certainly understand that. "I reckon we need to get him out of there pronto."

McCracken nodded.

"You given any thought as to how we're gonna accomplish that?"

"Reckon I'll just take you out there, introduce you to Hank, and let you handle things from there."

Law pondered that for a few moments, then shook his head. He said, "Sounds kind of dangerous to me."

"How so?"

"Well, if Kuykendall has as many men as you say he does, they're probably gonna be keepin' an eye on the roads in and out of Big Spring. By now, everyone 'round here knows I'm here. Kuykendall's men see you and somebody like me ridin' out of here and goin' to some farm, they're gonna be suspicious as hell. And, if any of those boys has any brains a'tall—which I ain't sayin' they do—or if they get back here and talk with Kuykendall, they'll just set out there and wait for this Blackstone to come out in the open and gun him down."

"Damn," McCracken snapped. "You got any suggestions?"

"I suppose you could just make me a map to the farm and I could go on out there myself."

"Won't work," the sheriff said with a shake of the head. He rolled a cigarette as he talked. "The people there wouldn't trust you. I don't know that they'd even trust you if I sent a letter with you. They'd just fear you were one of Kuykendall's men and maybe forged the letter. Or forced me to write it somehow. And even if these folk were inclined to believe it, I'm not sure Hank would feel the same. He'd as like bolt as not."

"Does leave us with a quandary, don't it?" Law commented.

"It does."

They sat in silence for a bit, then Law said, "How about this, Jess?"

CHAPTER 7

✶

LAW SHOOK HANDS farewell with his old friend Jesse McCracken on the wood sidewalk in front of the sheriff's office. Then he ambled down Main Street to Third Street, then west to O'Fallon's livery.

Sean O'Fallon greeted him with a boozy hello. "Leavin' town already, Mr. Law?" he asked, his brogue mostly undiluted by whiskey as it was yet early in the morning.

"I am. I'd be obliged if you'd saddle and bridle Toby for me."

O'Fallon stared at him for a moment with bleary eyes, then turned and headed into the barn. He returned a few minutes later with Toby in tow. The big buckskin seemed pleased to see his master. Law patted the animal's head, then slipped him a lump of sugar. Law paid O'Fallon, then mounted the horse and rode back to the Llano House. There he picked up his saddlebags and rifle from his room, checked out—McCracken had already made arrangements for payment—and then rode across the street to Wentworth's. He tied Toby to the hitching rail just off the sidewalk and went inside.

Dillman's body was gone, and someone had spread some sawdust and hay over the bloodstain.

"Mr. Law," the old man said, offering a small, worried smile. "Welcome back. You forgot your cigars."

"One of the reasons I'm back," Law allowed. "I also need a few supplies, since I'm leavin' town."

"Be glad to help." He hesitated. "Especially after what you done for my grandson."

"How is the boy?"

"He'll be all right. Wouldn't have been, though, if it wasn't for you." He paused. "I don't know how to thank you."

"No need for thanks, Mr. . . ."

"Alva Wentworth. And I—"

"Like I said, Mr. Wentworth, there's no need for thanks. I ain't the kind of man to stand by while some damned thugs whale away on some child."

Wentworth moved off down the counter, picked up a handful of something, then returned to where Law stood. He opened his hand, and a dozen slim cigars rolled off and onto the counter. "These are free, Mr. Law," he said with more firmness than he had used in years. "And whatever else you need."

"I can't—"

"I insist." He crossed his scrawny arms over his thin chest, decision made.

Law stifled a smile. "I give in, Mr. Wentworth." He didn't need much in the way of supplies, and he would be spare about ordering what he did need. He could see no reason to take advantage of the man's gratitude.

"Good."

"I'll need a couple pounds of bacon, same of beans, a few taters, a couple of bags of coffee—Arbuckle's or any other kind you have on hand; I ain't particular—a bag of sugar, a bit of salt—"

"Some airtights?" Wentworth asked. "I have a variety of items in cans."

Law shook his head. "I don't have a packhorse, Mr. Wentworth, nor do I intend to get one. I travel light. Airtights're tasty things to have along at times, but they do carry a lot of weight."

"Sensible." Wentworth paused a moment, thinking, then said, "Well, if airtights're no good, I would suggest some beef jerky. A couple of pounds won't add much weight, and they'll last a good long time if husbanded."

Law nodded.

Wentworth moved off and came back with several small sacks. "Anything else I can get for you, Mr. Law?" he asked almost eagerly.

"Just some tobacco, papers, and lucifers."

Those items soon joined the small stash on the counter. "You sure I can't pay you somethin' for all this?" Law asked as he pulled a sheaf of greenbacks from an inside coat pocket.

"I'm certain," Wentworth said with finality.

Law put the money away.

"Need any help carrying this outside?" Wentworth asked.

Law shook his head. "There ain't that much, and my horse is right outside."

"Still," Wentworth said, sweeping up most of the supplies in his arms, "you'll need your hands free to pack your saddlebags."

"Obliged." Law stuffed the cigars in his inner breast pocket, and the tobacco, papers and matches in outside pockets, then turned and headed outside. Within minutes, with Wentworth's help, he had his meager supplies jammed into his saddlebags.

"Well, Mr. Wentworth," Law said as he pulled himself into the saddle, "I'm obliged for everything."

"No, sir, it's me who owes you," the old man insisted. "You ever need anything and you're in these parts, you come see ol' Alva Wentworth. Even if you got no cash. You come see me. Wasn't for you, me and my grandson'd be deader'n a door-nail, like as not. Now you travel safe, Mr. Law."

The bounty man grinned at Wentworth and touched the brim of his flat-crowned hat by way of farewell. He rode leisurely southeast down Main Street, going back the way he had entered the town the day before.

When he had gotten two miles outside of town, by his estimate, he pulled off the road and headed cross-country. He topped a rise on the treeless plain about a hundred yards off the road and stopped at the bottom. He ground staked Toby, then removed his frock coat and vest and slid them under the thong tying his bedroll to the saddle's cantle. Then he grabbed his wood canteen, collapsible telescope, and two pieces of jerky, and walked to the top of the rise and sat.

Law gnawed at a strip of jerky, silently cursing the brutal sun and the insufferable temperature as he kept an eye on the road, especially the direction to Big Spring. Just sitting there, with the heat pounding down on his head and shoulders made Law sleepy, and he had to fight to stay awake. He managed, though it was not easy.

Just after two almost intolerable hours, he saw a cloud of dust coming from the direction of Big Spring. He perked up, alert. Soon he could see two specks on the road. He waited a few more minutes, then pulled out his telescope and trained it on the riders. They were moving at a good clip. As they neared, Law could see that they were hard cases—each had tied-down guns and did not have even the least bit of a friendly look about him.

Swinging his telescope the other way, Law spotted a small stand of mesquite mixed with scrubby shin oak and skunkbush sumac. He nodded, snapped the telescope shut, and hurried down the hill. He climbed into the saddle and set Toby off at a trot around the rise, southeast, away from the town. At the mesquites just off the road, he stopped and tied Toby to a tree. He walked a few feet away, trying to find what shade he could, and waited.

It was not long before the two riders came into view. They slowed as soon as they saw the trees, and slowed even more when they spotted Toby placidly munching the buffalo grass. They stopped when Law stepped out from amid the trees.

"Lookin' for somebody?" Law asked quietly. He stood with feet slightly apart, thumbs in his gun belt.

"Nope," the one man said. He wore a new gray hat with a high, deeply creased crown, which shadowed his face.

"We're just moseyin' on down to San Angelo," the second added. Like the other, he was dressed in worn denim pants and a faded shirt of nondescript color. But he wore a leather vest with fancy gold buttons.

"You're runnin' them horses pretty hard in this heat for a couple of boys supposed to be just moseyin'," Law noted.

"That's none of your concern, asshole," Big Hat said with a snarl.

Law sucked in a breath, then eased it out. He was tired of such men. "Look, boys," he said evenly, "I got no beef with y'all. So, if you know what's good for you, you'll just turn them horses around and head back to Big Spring. That'd be the wise thing to do."

Though Law didn't much think they were smart enough to take the suggestion, he continued, "And when you get back there, you can tell Kuykendall to leave me the hell alone."

"Who?" Gold Buttons offered.

"You really are dumb as a rock, ain't you, boy," Law commented, managing to keep a straight face. "You can just tell him that I do not take kindly to some skunk like him sendin' cockroaches like you two to annoy me. Tell him it ain't necessary— and it ain't goin' to do him any good."

"That ain't what Mr. Kuykendall says," Big Hat said. He waved a hand cutting off Gold Buttons's protests. "He don't believe us that we don't know Mr. Kuykendall," he said to his companion. "Besides, he ain't gonna live long enough to cause no trouble." He turned back to Law and gave him a sneering grin.

"You boys're about to make a big mistake," Law said calmly. "But it doesn't have to end badly for you. Just turn your horses and ride on out of here." He was sure they would not heed his advice.

He was right. The two men pretended as if they were going to turn around but then went for their weapons. Gold Buttons drew fast and fired twice, then a third time. But his speed made him wild, and all three bullets went flying off to nowhere.

Law unlimbered the Peacemaker from the belt holster and brought the weapon up, as he went into a crouch. He calmly squeezed off two shots. One hit Gold Buttons in the throat; the other in the chest. He wavered in the saddle for a moment, then fell backward, hanging there awkwardly with both boots still in the stirrups.

Gold Buttons's horse shuffled at the unusual activity on its back, bumping into the other mount just as Big Hat hauled out his Smith and Wesson. The animal jerked as Big Hat fired, sending the bullet whistling off into the trees to Law's left.

Law swung toward him and fired, but the horse's continued movement as it nervously shuffled threw the bounty man's aim off as well. He did manage to hit Big Hat, but only in the right shoulder.

Big Hat dropped his pistol. He reflexively bent, as if trying to get it, so Law's next shot passed over him. His horse, already spooked, bucked, throwing Big Hat to the ground. He landed with a thud and a grunt in the grass.

Before Big Hat could recover, Law trotted up and placed a boot sole on his right forearm, making sure he could not get at the pistol.

"Why'd Kuykendall send you two damn fools after me?" Law asked, aiming his cocked Colt at Big Hat's forehead.

"He heard from some of the boys that you was cozyin' up to the sheriff. And, since you killed Clem and Wally and the others, we—well, Mr. Kuykendall—figured you was in cahoots with that son of a bitch McCracken."

It made sense to Law. If he was Kuykendall, he would have had the same thoughts and sent someone after the man he suspected of helping the law dog who was trying to get him hanged.

"There anyone else comin' after me besides you and your idiot pard over there?" Law asked.

"Nope," Big Hat answered. "Mr. Kuykendall didn't figure me and Georgie would have any trouble." He grimaced, partly from the pain of his wound, partly from shame.

"Figured wrong, didn't he," Law said more than asked. He took a deep breath and let it out slowly. He ought to just put a bullet in this man's brain and be done with it, he knew. But that went against the grain with him. "Well," he finally said, "I don't present any danger to Kuykendall. Unless he sends someone else after me. So you got a choice, bub. You can give me your word you'll not come against me, and that you'll head on back to Big Spring and stay there, tellin' Kuykendall to leave me alone."

"Or?" Big Hat wondered aloud, though he knew.

Law gave him a raised eyebrow, as if saying, *You know damn well what.*

Big Hat nodded once, then let his head go back and rest on the ground. After a moment, he said, "I give you my word, pard. I'll go on back to Big Spring and tell Mr. Kuykendall you're not gonna cause him no trouble."

Law considered that for several seconds. He really didn't believe the man, but he had to give him the chance. He nodded and slid the Colt back into the holster. He took his foot off Big Hat's arm, then knelt and picked up the man's revolver, which he tossed back into the mesquite trees after taking several steps back.

"You want to take your friend there back to town with you, you're gonna have to tie him on his horse lest he go tumblin' off while you're ridin'," Law said.

"Reckon that ain't gonna be easy with my arm all boogered up like it is," Big Hat said.

"That's your lookout, bub," Law allowed.

Big Hat nodded and moved to the horse, which was still skittish. He grabbed the reins and calmed the animal, then took the coiled rope tied to the front of the saddle. Working gingerly and slowly because of his shoulder wound, he began trying to loop the rope under the horse's belly and over his companion's body. He frequently glanced over his shoulder as he proceeded, keeping an eye on Law.

The bounty man watched for a bit, then drifted off toward Toby to make sure the horse had not been hit by any stray bullets. Though he did not appear to be paying any attention to Big Hat, he was, in fact, aware of every move the man made.

Big Hat slowed even more in his work, barely moving as he pretended to tie a final knot in the rope. With the horse blocking his movements from Law, Big Hat slid his hand into one of Georgie's saddlebags. Suddenly he jerked out the spare pistol he knew was there, shoved past the horse's rump, and cocked the revolver as he brought it to bear on Law, whose back was toward him.

CHAPTER 8

✦

LAW, WHO HAD been expecting Big Hat to try something, spun and dropped to one knee, drawing the Peacemaker when he heard Big Hat cock the pistol. Big Hat managed to fire first, but the bullet went where Law no longer was.

"Goddamn fool," Law muttered as he plugged the now hatless Big Hat twice, the two lead bullets in the heart smashing him to the ground in a bloody sprawl.

Law rose and walked warily to where Big Hat lay. He put his Colt away when he was sure the man was dead. For a few moments, he contemplated what to do, being predisposed to just leaving the bodies right where they were. But he decided that wouldn't be very pleasant to see if a stage came along with some women or children as passengers.

He grabbed one of Big Hat's wrists and dragged the corpse back into the trees and left it there. Then he led Gold Buttons's horse back there and stopped where he had left Big Hat. With the big blade of his hunting knife, he sliced the ropes lashing Gold Buttons to the horse. He tugged the body off and let it fall to the ground next to Big Hat.

Law went through the saddlebags on that horse but found little of use or interest—except a pint bottle of bad whiskey. He decided to keep that and slipped it into his own saddlebags. He led the horse out onto the road, facing away from Big Spring. "Go on, git!" he suddenly shouted, swatting the animal on the rump with a calloused hand.

The horse bolted, and Law stood there for a few moments watching it race away, just to make sure it didn't stop. He would've preferred sending the steed back to town, but then someone might come looking for its owner, and he did not need that right now. He figured someone would come along after a while and spot the animal, or it would stop running soon and start grazing and eventually be taken back to Big Spring—if not taken home by some farmer or rancher.

It took several minutes—during which Law got increasingly frustrated with the heat broiling him—to calm Big Hat's horse down enough to get close to it. When he did, he checked those saddlebags, too, finding nothing that he thought worth keeping. Then he took that horse onto the road and with a good smack, sent it racing after Gold Buttons's mount.

Law walked back to Toby and drank deeply from the wood canteen, then wiped sweat off his forehead on a shirtsleeve. He climbed into the saddle and moved Toby out around from behind the trees. He stopped on the road and looked back. The bodies of Big Hat and Gold Buttons were still visible, but at least they were not out in the open. Somebody would find them sooner or later.

He touched his bootheels to Toby's side and moved off across the road and onto the prairie, heading cross-country again in a generally westerly direction.

A couple of hours later, he found Sheriff Jesse McCracken sitting in the meager shade provided by a gnarly, wind-twisted mesquite tree. He stopped and dismounted, lightly tying Toby's reins to the tree next to McCracken's horse. He loosened Toby's saddle to let the animal breathe. Taking the pint of whiskey and the canteen of water, he plopped himself down on the dry, brittle grama grass next to his friend.

"Sure took you long enough to git here, pard," McCracken said dryly.

"Had a slight detour." Using his teeth, Law pulled the cork out of the bottle and took a sip before handing it to McCracken.

"Oh?" the sheriff asked, one eyebrow cocked in question.

Law explained what had happened.

McCracken sat silently during the recollection, sipping whiskey as he and Law passed the bottle back and forth. "Know who they were?" McCracken asked when Law was through.

"Nope." He pulled out two cigars, handed one to McCracken, and then lit both of them on a match. He described the two, adding, "The one called the other Georgie. That's about as close to a name as I got for either of them."

"Sounds like Georgie Overmeyer and Chase McGarrigle," McCracken commented. "Lovely couple of fellers, just like the rest of Kuykendall's devilish gunmen. I got paper on 'em, but not for anything important. I know they've killed at least half a dozen people each, but I can't prove it. What reward is offered for 'em don't amount to beans and ain't worth anyone's effort to collect. But I'll see you get whatever reward there is."

"Obliged," Law said flatly. "Gotta pay for the bullets I used on those cockroaches."

"I'll have someone go on out and pick 'em up soon's I get back to Big Spring. Or," he added after a moment's thought, "maybe I'll just mosey on over there on the way back and save some effort."

"Best go to town first," Law said. "I sent their horses packin', and I doubt those animals would've wandered back to stand watch over their late, unlamented masters."

McCracken nodded. "That could be a problem," he said. "People see me or one of my deputies headin' out with a couple of horses or a wagon, tongues'll start waggin'. Especially when I come back with a couple of Kuykendall's boys dead. People're gonna wonder how I knew where they were—or knew enough to bring some horses out there."

Law shrugged. He figured McCracken would come up with some story if anyone in town questioned him on it. "Hell, go on over that way now and head back into town that way. Anybody asks, you can just tell 'em you saw the bodies out there on your jaunt to wherever you told 'em you were going, and came back to town to get a wagon to take 'em back."

"That might work," McCracken mused, unconcerned about it all.

Law stared out across the sun-blasted prairie for a few minutes, then finished off the last of the whiskey and tossed the bottle out into the grass. "You have any trouble on the way out here, Jess?" he finally asked.

"Not a speck. Just moseyed on like I often do, and no one paid me no nevermind a'tall. I did stop for a short spell just to make sure nobody was followin' me, but apparently no one gave much of a damn." He sounded almost wistful, as if he had wanted someone to have followed him so he could've had some action, like Law had had.

McCracken rose, brushing off the seat of his pants. "Well, John Thomas, we best get movin'. Still some ground to cover and things to be done."

Law stood, too, amazed again at how much he towered over his friend. Yes, despite McCracken's lack of height, there were few men Law would rather have at his side in a battle.

As they mounted their horses and moved off, Law asked, "Where're we headin', Jess?"

"Farmhouse a couple of miles on yonder. The farmer's name is Lucas Drummond. His wife's name is Winnifred Willoughby." He glanced at Law, who was staring at him in question. "My brother-in-law—Winnifred is Lucy Mae's sister. Well, half sister."

Law nodded. "Well, I reckon that's reason enough to be willin' to take Blackstone in for a spell." Law didn't believe that for a minute. It wasn't as if this Drummond was really family.

"Not according to Winnifred, that's for sure. She was dead set against it right from the start." He tried to smile, but it came out more like a grimace.

"Can't say as I'd blame her for that, Jess," Law allowed. "It's mighty dangerous for that family. Hell, if Kuykendall found out Blackstone was there . . ."

"I know, I know," McCracken snapped. "Lawd a'mighty, J.T., I've heard it constant not only from Winnifred whenever I'm in earshot of her, but also from Lucy Mae every second of the day it seems."

"Then why?"

"Had no place else to put him. It just so happened that Luke was in Big Spring when we were tryin' to decide what to do with Blackstone right at the start. Luke came by the office and heard what we was talkin' about. He suggested hidin' Blackstone out at his farm. I thought he was loco, 'cause I knew what Winnifred—she don't favor bein' called Winnie, by the way, just so's you know—was gonna say about it. And, hell, I could understand it. Was it me in Luke's position, I don't know as if I would've offered to help, family or not."

"Sure you would've, Jess," Law said quietly. "It's just the kind of man you are."

McCracken offered up a grunt, embarrassed that he could be seen by some as such a softhearted man.

Law knew what his friend was thinking and added, "It takes a tough man to put his wife and youngsters in danger to help out kinfolk who're in dire straits, pard."

"I reckon. Can't see it for myself, but it's sure as hell true for Luke. He's tough as any man I ever saw but still has a good heart. I mean, it ain't like he's kin to me." He offered up a small chuckle. "You want to hear somethin' completely *loco*?" he asked rhetorically. He glanced slyly at Law, who was paying full attention.

"Luke's a damn Yankee!" McCracken said with a combination of humor and bafflement. "You believe that? A goddamn Yankee. Fought for the Union side in the Late Unpleasantness."

Law thought he did a fairly good job of hiding his shock—and irritation.

"He don't talk about it much, but from what he has said, he faced some damned hard times fightin' against our boys. Winnifred come out one day while we was visitin' and said that he should show me his medals. I thought he was gonna go apoplectic on me right then and there. He apologized for his wife's ill-considered suggestion, and he's never brought it up again. Hell, for that matter, he don't bring up the war a'tall and tries to talk about somethin' else if someone else does."

"Sounds like a good man," Law said grudgingly.

"A damn fine one," McCracken said adamantly. "I'm right proud to call him family now, and I'll gut any man takes exception to that—or to him." He glared at Law.

The bounty man stared back for some moments, then smiled a little. "If you think he's that good a man, Jess, that's good enough for me. I might not like Yankees in general, but I have met a few I can abide." He paused, then asked, "How'd he get to a farm out here?"

"The Bluebellies in charge sent him down here afterward, and he took a likin' to the place, especially after meetin' Winnifred." He paused, shaking his head. "What he ever saw in that woman, I'll never know," he muttered.

"Hell, she can't be all bad if she's a Texas gal," Law said with a small laugh.

"Reckon you're right, J.T., but I swear she can be mighty tryin' at times. There's times I can't even believe she's Lucy Mae's sister. Them two're like the sun and the moon—opposite in just about every way. Might be that she's some years older than Lucy Mae." He shook his head again, still wondering at the strangeness of life. "Anyway, Luke mustered out soon after, married Winnifred, found this land out here, and settled down." He turned sharp eyes on Law again. "But he ain't no carpet-bagger," he insisted. "Never was. If he was, I'd of never been able to tolerate him."

Law was interested in meeting Luke Drummond. If he was half the man McCracken was painting him out to be, he would be a welcome friend. "Seems even more dangerous for you to stick Blackstone here," he said. "I mean, if Kuykendall was to find out that Luke's wife is your wife's sister . . ."

"Another reason I was hopin' you'd get here in a hurry. It ain't likely that Kuykendall or his hired guns would hear about that relationship, but sometimes things get out. Of course, we thought about that when we first talked about keepin' Blackstone here for a few days. We finally decided that even if Kuykendall somehow found out about the relationship, he'd figure that me and Luke would never put our families in so much danger as to have a witness—the only damn witness—against Kuykendall stay here."

"Well, it seems to have worked out." Law wasn't having worries about having taken on this job so much as he was second thoughts. The relationship between Jess McCracken and Luke Drummond, even if only through marriage, could be just another complication in this whole affair. And any complication could be dangerous for Law and for Hank Blackstone.

The two men rode on in silence then for a while, suffering with the heat and their own thoughts.

Finally McCracken poked Law in the arm with an elbow, and then pointed. "Almost there," he said.

Off in the distance, law could make out—barely—the blades of a windmill.

In ten minutes they had passed the windmill, which creaked loudly in the steady, hot breeze. And then they were pulling up in front of a neat little farmhouse with a full porch across the front, which faced roughly east. Flowers, now struggling to survive in the heat and sun, were planted along the front of the porch, except at the steps. From out back, Law could hear pigs, chickens, and goats. A lowing announced the presence of one, maybe two, milk cows. A well-tended garden plot stretched a few yards out from the south side of the house. A sliver of water ran from somewhere behind the house on a diagonal, past the garden patch and off toward the southeast. Fifty feet or so from the north side of the house sat a barn.

A quite pregnant but still pinch-faced woman in a drab cotton dress and apron spread across her bulging belly stepped out of the door of the house onto the porch. She shaded her eyes with a hand. "Jesse? That you?" she called out.

"Yes, Winnifred," McCracken said with a portentous sigh as he dismounted.

"Well it's nigh on time you got here," she said, moving forward to the top step. "We can't be keepin' an eye on that man for you forever, you know. Luke's almighty busy most times and . . ."

CHAPTER 9

✳

"Winnifred," McCracken said loudly, to get her to shut up, "this is John Thomas Law. He's here to help us."

"Help you, you mean," Winnifred insisted. "We're done helpin' you with this, Jess. It's much too dangerous for all of us, and mighty tryin', I'll tell you. I don't know how Lucy—"

"Where's Luke?" Law interrupted.

"Out in the field. Where else would he be at this time of day? I swear, Jess, you don't stop to think very often. You just—"

"Go send Jasper out to fetch him back here, please," McCracken said.

"Jasper's out with his pa, as you'd know if you used any of the sense the Good Lord gave you, Jesse McCracken. Out here on the farm, we have lots to keep us busy, not like you towns-folk who—"

"Then send Harold or," he plowed ahead hastily, lest he give Winnifred another opening, "Eldon, if Harold ain't here."

Watching the exchange, Law wondered how the sheriff kept so calm. McCracken had not been lying when he had said that Winnifred was a trying woman.

Without waiting to hear any more from Winnifred, Mc-Cracken turned and walked, leading his horse, to the water pump. Law was right beside him. McCracken jerked the pump handle up and down several times until water splashed out into the small trough below the spout. When the trough was half full, the two men let the horses drink. The thirsty animals went through the water pretty quickly, so Law pumped more in.

When the mounts had had their fill, McCracken held the reins to both and indicated with a jerk of the head that Law should go next. Law bent over, mouth near the spout, and pumped more water, gulping it down greedily. Then he stepped around and knelt at the trough, dropping his hat next to him. He plunged his head into the cool water, then snapped it back out, whipping his thick mane of black hair back and forth, reveling in the invigorating coolness of the liquid on his head, face, and neck.

Then he took the reins to the horses and let McCracken refresh himself. As he stood there, Law saw a boy of six or seven running across the prairie behind the house.

McCracken noticed the boy, too. "That's Eldon," he said. "Next to the youngest. Jasper, the oldest, is eleven; then there's Harold, who's nine, I think; Rachel, who's almost eight; Eldon there, he's six; and Leah, the baby for the time being, who's three."

"Nice little family," Law said dryly.

McCracken gave him a withering glance, then said, "Let's go get the horses over into the barn out of this damn sun and heat."

They walked slowly toward the barn, McCracken casting glances at the house. Winnifred remained on the porch, watching them. Before the two men had gotten far, however, Winnifred had turned and gone back in the house, much to McCracken's obvious relief.

As they entered the barn, McCracken called out, "Hank. Hank Blackstone. You in here?"

There was no response.

McCracken shrugged. "I didn't reckon he'd be here, but I thought I'd check," he offered. "I reckon he's out in the fields with Luke."

"Foolish," Law said. "He could be seen."

McCracken nodded. He agreed, but there was nothing he could do about it.

They unsaddled the horses and took off the bridles. Moving the animals into rough stalls, Law and McCracken pitchforked hay in for the horses, then walked outside to wait.

Law once more pulled out two cigars, passing one to Mc-Cracken. He held out a lit match for the sheriff, then put the flame to his own cigar.

"You ever think of settling down, J.T.?" McCracken asked. "I mean since turning into a bounty man?"

Law shrugged, uncomfortable with the question. "Reckon so," he finally offered. "At times anyway. But I figure such a thing ain't in the cards for a fella like me."

"Nothin' wrong with you, J.T. You're a handsome man—or at least I figure the ladies would think so—honest, hard-workin' . . ."

"Yep. Hardworkin'. Hardworkin' trackin' down bad men from one goddamn end of Texas to the other. That's real suit-able for settlin' down, ain't it."

"You could give it up, J.T.," McCracken said quietly. "I gave up the Rangers but still found suitable employment— a job that's secure, pays fairly well, and gives me enough excitement to keep life interestin'."

"Excitement, eh?" Law snorted. "Like frettin' over tryin' to keep a witness alive to testify against some miscreant who's been runnin' wild all over your county?"

"Well, hell, that ain't always been the case," McCracken said ruefully. "Usually things're pretty calm around here."

"Can't have been too calm with Kuykendall runnin' loose," Law said reasonably.

McCracken spat out a piece of tobacco. "Bah, sorry I brought it up," he growled. "I was just lookin' out for your future. You can't do this forever, you know, J.T."

"I know." There was resignation in Law's voice.

"You ought to consider givin' it up before it kills you, boy." He almost managed a smile. "We could use a town marshal in Big Spring."

"That's somethin' to cogitate on," Law said dryly. "I'd die of boredom instead of battlin' some desperate desperado."

Both laughed.

More silence, then Law commented, "You weren't stretchin' things when you indicated Winnifred was a harridan."

McCracken half-smiled, half-grimaced. "All I can say is that it's a good thing Luke's married to her and not me. If I was married to her, I figure I'd end up putting a bullet in one or the other of us." He chuckled. "And I ain't so sure which!"

Law blew out a stream of smoke when he laughed. "I reckon I'd feel about the same." He paused, then said, "One of these days I'm gonna have to meet your Lucy Mae, just to make sure you weren't lyin' to me about her and Winnifred bein' opposites. I'd sure hate to think you'd lost your reason and married someone like that one in that farmhouse over there."

"If I had, I would've shot myself already."

Before Law could respond, he and McCracken saw two men and three boys hurrying across the plains toward the house. The two lawmen moved away from the barn, and McCracken waved. One of the men crossing the prairie waved back. "That'd be Luke," McCracken said.

The two groups met, and the man who had waved nodded greetings at McCracken and Law. Then he said to the three youngsters, "You boys go on in the house now. Or go cool yourselves over at the pump first."

"But, Pa—" Jasper started.

"Don't sass me, boy," Drummond said sternly. But there was an undertone of caring in his voice. "Now go on and do as you're told. We men here have business to discuss."

The three boys headed off, the youngest, Eldon, happily skipping along, not worried in the least about adult business. The oldest, Jasper, glanced over his shoulder a few times, wistfully. He wanted to be included in adult discussions, even though he wasn't sure he would understand much of what would be said. He didn't like being eleven. He was too old to be a child like Eldon, or even Harold, yet not old enough to be considered grown-up. When he was within a few feet of the pump, Harold suddenly scooped up a hatful of water from the trough and flung it at him. He forgot about adult pursuits as he went to join the water battle with his brothers.

"Luke, Hank," McCracken said, "this is John Thomas Law. He's here to keep you safe until the trial, Hank."

The three men shook hands.

"Glad to meet you, Mr. Law," Blackstone said.

"Call me J.T. Or John Thomas, if you're of a mind to," Law said, while taking stock of his new charge.

Blackstone was a man about a decade younger than Law—maybe his mid-twenties—of medium height, stocky, with a broad, pale face. Faded blue eyes stared out from under straw-colored eyebrows and over a long, slightly crooked nose and thin lips. He seemed permanently frightened and worried. And he had a haunted look deep in his eyes. Yellowish stubble covered his cheeks and chin, and a knot of hair the same color as the eyebrows hung down from under the back of a worn but serviceable wide-brimmed hat with a tall, round crown.

"So, what do we do first, Mr. . . . um, J.T.?" Blackstone asked.

"Well, we're gonna need some supplies," Law said, "since we won't be able to get into town much—if at all."

"I ain't goin' inter Big Spring no way, no how," Blackstone insisted. "Not while that sumbitch's men are still roamin' free."

"Nor would I expect you to," Law said. "So we'll need supplies to tide us over."

"That's where you come in, Luke," McCracken said. "We need you to ride on into town and get what supplies J.T. needs."

"When?"

"Right now."

"I'll need some grub first," Drummond said firmly. "I ain't workin' all mornin' out in the field there, then ridin' all the way into Big Spring to pick up a pile of supplies and then ride back here on an empty stomach."

McCracken smiled and nodded. "I could use with some feedin' myself," he noted.

During the exchange between the two, Law had observed Drummond. He was a big man, solid but turning a little to flab. When he took off his sun-bleached brown slouch hat, he revealed a balding pate rimmed on sides and back with stringy reddish brown hair. A bushy, white-flecked beard covered the bottom half of his face. A fleshy nose dominated his sunbeaten face.

"I expect Winnifred'll have something ready," Drummond said. He turned and headed for the house, the others moving along with him. All stopped at the trough to wash up a little—or at least get some of the dust off their hands, faces, and necks.

As the men entered the house, the children, each carrying a loaded plate, started filing out onto the porch and taking places at a table there. Then the men went in and sat at the well-kept table.

"There's plenty there, so eat up," Winnifred said as she set platters loaded with pork chops and corn dodgers on the table. She went to the large cast-iron stove and returned with a platter of biscuits and a large bowl of snap beans. "After all, Mr. Blackstone and him"—she nodded at Law—"will need to have full bellies when they ride on out of here right after you all—"

"That's enough, woman," Drummond said sharply. "Mr. Blackstone and Mr. Law will leave when it's right for them to do so."

"But, Luke—"

"Enough, I said. We have business to discuss, and we don't need your musings while we're doin' so. The food's on the table. You may join us if you wish—and if you keep your peace. If not, or if you're not of a mind to eat with us, then find yourself some chores to do. There's no dearth of work that needs to be done."

Law waited for a screeching response, and was surprised—no, more like shocked—when she nodded.

"Yes, dear," she said almost meekly. "Do you need anything else?"

"Just the coffeepot here on the table," Drummond said. His voice had softened.

Law glanced at McCracken, who shook his head in befuddlement. "I ain't ever seen the like," the sheriff whispered. "He ain't ever done that in front of me before."

Law decided that eating was a good idea. He was hungry as a starving wolf anyway, and the aroma of the steaming pork chops was enticing. He loaded up his plate, grabbed a couple of biscuits, and dug in.

When the eating was well under way, Drummond asked, "So what will you need for supplies, Mr. Law—er, J.T.?"

"Bacon, beans, salt, coffee, salt beef," Law replied around bites of food. He looked at Blackstone. "You any kind of cook, Mr. Blackstone?"

"Only when forced into it," Blackstone said dully. "I can muster up corn pone when need be, and I have a decent hand with some Mexican dishes of beans and spices."

Law nodded, looking back at Drummond. "Best get some cornmeal then, and some flour." He grinned a little. "I can manage biscuits. Sometimes." He paused, then added, "And see what Mr. Blackstone—"

"Hank," Blackstone insisted.

Law bobbed his head. "See what spices Hank there might want." He paused again, thinking and chewing. "You do have a horse for Hank, don't you, Jess?" he asked.

"Well, damn, no," McCracken said. His annoyance at his lack of forethought was immediate and strong. "I never thunk of that."

"How'd you get him here in the first place?" Law questioned.

"Back of a wagon," McCracken responded with a grin. "Under a pile of canvas and rambunctious children."

Law fought back a smile. "Well, then, Jess, we'll need a horse and saddle for Hank. And we probably ought to have a mule or another horse for packin' supplies. I don't intend to stay in one spot too long, so we'll be on the move regular. I don't intend to have Toby burdened down with a heap of supplies."

McCracken nodded. But he did not look happy. "I got to figure out how Luke can bring a horse and mule or a couple of horses back from Big Spring without no one gittin' too suspicious."

"A farmer getting a horse and a mule shouldn't raise too many eyebrows," Drummond threw in.

"Maybe not," McCracken allowed.

"I would figure, though, that it might be better if I just got two mules. No one'd think the worse for me bringin' two mules back here. And Hank could manage to ride a mule, I'd think."

"That's a fact," McCracken said. Then added, "But buyin' up the tack that goes with ridin' might be seen as some strange for a farmer known for comin' into town with his wagon all the time. Besides, I ain't sure I'd be able to come up with the cash you'd need to make the purchases. Not on short notice anyway."

They ate in silence, pondering this latest conundrum. Suddenly Law allowed a grin to start stretching across his face. "I think I might have me an idea on rectifyin' this situation," he said.

CHAPTER 10

WITH THE EYES of all the others on him, Law asked, "How far's Kuykendall's ranch from here?"

"Four, file miles across the prairie, I reckon," the sheriff answered, looking at Law in question. "Another reason we thought of keepin' Hank here for a short while—figured Kuykendall'd never think we'd put him so close to the devil's own house. Why?"

"You said he had a passel of horses—often out in the open," Law said. It was mostly a question.

"True, but . . ." McCracken's eyes suddenly widened, then he began to grin. "Good goddamn, take a couple of horses from that son of a bitch, right out from under his men's noses," he said with a burst of enthusiasm. Suddenly he looked around, worried about his language when he remembered there was a woman around. But Winnifred was still outside on the porch, and he relaxed.

Law nodded. "Yep, old friend." He grinned again. "'Course, I wouldn't expect you to go along on this particular outin'," he added. "After all, we'd be stealin'."

"Stealin', hell," McCracken snorted. "I expect most every horse on that ranch was stole from somebody else. You ain't keepin' me out of this little venture."

"I figured you'd feel that way," Law noted with just a touch of smugness.

"I'm in, too," Drummond said with determination.

McCracken shook his head. "Nope, Luke. You still need to go to town, and this here action'll be purty dangerous."

"Besides," Law added, "you got no way to get there—unless you plan to ride one of your plowin' mules bareback. And that'd take us a week of Sundays to get there."

Drummond nodded glumly.

"What about me?" Blackstone asked.

"You'll have to stay here," McCracken said.

Blackstone accepted it, relieved. He was not a fighting man and had a healthy enough fear of Chester Kuykendall and his men already. He did not need to tempt fate any more than he was already doing.

The men hurried through the rest of the meal, though they forced themselves to relax a little, taking the time to have a smoke with coffee afterward. Then they were ready to prepare for their missions.

"You need us to write down those supplies we need, Luke?" Law asked as the men watched Winnifred clean off the table.

Drummond shook his head. "I'll remember," he grumbled, still put out that he would not be in on the raid against Kuykendall's ranch. It had been a long time since he had really tested his mettle in battle, and he missed it. Or at least he thought he did when he was not allowed to take part in any of it.

Drummond scratched his bushy beard. "Anythin' else I can do for you fellows before I get on my way?" he asked.

"You got some paper?" McCracken asked. "And a pencil that's useable?"

"Reckon I got something around." Drummond said flatly. He took pride in his ability to read and write, and he always kept plenty of paper—and pen and ink—in the house for writing letters or just the events of the day when it struck him to do so.

He rose and went into the back room, which he and Winnifred shared, and returned several minutes later with some

foolscap and two stubby pencils. He laid them on the table.
He sighed deeply, letting out the anger at not being involved
in the raid. Each man had his own things to do, and that was
not his. He would not leave his brother-in-law and new friend
with poor feelings to mar their mission.

"You two fellows take care of yourself on this adventure,
understand?" he said gruffly.

McCracken and Law nodded.

"You be careful in Big Spring, Luke," McCracken said.
"Just go on in, get the supplies, and git out."

Drummond nodded. "I do not plan to dawdle, Jess." He
headed for the door, shouting, "Jasper, come and help me hitch
up the wagon."

McCracken grabbed one of the sheets of paper and a pencil.
Standing and bending over the table, he swiftly made some
sketches. "Now this here is Kuykendall's house," he said, pointing with the tip of the pencil. "The barn is here between the two
bunkhouses his gunmen use. And this is the bunkhouse for
his ranch hands. The main herd of horses could be anywhere
within two miles of the ranch house in any direction. He has his
boys move them pretty often so they always have fresh grass."

"Considerate," Law said sarcastically.

McCracken ignored the comment. "So we might have to
search awhile to find them."

"To hell with that," Law interjected. "Kuykendall might have
his men keep most of the horses out on the prairie, but there's
got to be a fair number in the barn, ready for his men to use at a
moment's notice. There'd also be tack in the barn. That's where
we need to go, instead of searchin' all over God's creation for a
bunch of horses that'll like as not be well guarded."

"And the barn won't be well guarded?" McCracken countered.

"I doubt the barn'll be guarded a'tall, really," Law said
evenly. "Don't mean there won't be a passel of hard cases all
around. We'll just have to deal with them as we can."

"Twenty, thirty guns?" McCracken asked skeptically.

"Hell, Jess, we faced worse odds than that many a time
when we was riding with Quantrill, and then Bill Anderson
when Quantrill bought the farm."

"That's true," McCracken acknowledged.

"And, like I said, we ain't got forever to do what we need to do. We just need to grab us a couple of horses and some tack and get the hell out. We can't go searchin' for horses out on the prairie. Besides, even if we found them fairly quick off, we'd still have to raid that barn to get a saddle and bridle and all."

McCracken nodded curtly, accepting the wisdom of it.

"Now, I ain't sayin'," Law added, "that if we find them horses right there in front of us while we're headin' toward the ranch that we can't take a couple of 'em and then worry about the gear."

"Agreed. When do we leave?"

"Couple of hours, I reckon," Law said after a moment's thought. "Let Toby and your horse get a bit more rest. Besides, I don't want to get there in the daylight. We'll need the cover of darkness to do what we need to if the place is as much out in the open as I suspect it is."

"Oh, it's out in the open all right," McCracken said with a nod. "Nothin' but prairie around it, though there is a good stand of cottonwoods along the crick near the house. Ain't nothin' to hide behind near the barn or bunkhouses, though."

The three men walked outside into the brutal sunshine. As they headed to the barn, Drummond drove his wagon, pulled by two mules, out of the structure. He stopped near the others. "Well, I'm on my way, boys. Good luck in your task."

"Same to you, Luke," McCracken said for himself, Law, and Blackstone.

Drummond snapped the reins, and the mules jerked the wagon forward, settling into a slow, steady pace.

The three other men continued to the barn. Inside, Law kicked some straw into a pile. He lay down on it and pulled his hat over his eyes. "I reckon a bit of shut-eye is in order," he said. In moments, he was asleep, not noticing his two companions doing the same.

LAW WAS THE first one awake, too. But even as he was tossing the saddle blanket onto Toby's back, McCracken arose, rubbing sleep from his face. The sheriff glanced at Blackstone, thinking he should wake the man, but then realized there was no reason to do that. So he went to saddle his own horse, a stout, strong, well-trained pinto.

Blackstone was still snoring softly when Law and McCracken rode out of the barn and across the flats, heading northwest.

"You ever think of goin' back to Missouri and clearin' up your trouble up there, J.T.?" McCracken asked as they rode.

"Can't say as I have, Jess," the bounty man responded. "I don't think that'd be a right good idea."

"They got some good lawmen up there, J.T., you should know that," McCracken said. "They'd take into account what you've been doin' all these past few years. And those things you done was a long time ago now."

"Won't make a gnat's bit of difference to them boys, I'd say. Not with Jesse and Cole and all the others still creatin' such a fuss all over the place like they been."

"I could put in a good word for you, J.T.," McCracken offered. "I'm sure Abe Covington'd be proud to do the same. The word of a county sheriff and a well-thought-of Texas Ranger's bound to carry a heap of weight, even with them boys up there."

"I'll keep it to mind, Jess," Law said seriously. He had never really given much thought to going to Missouri and Kansas to try to clear his name. He really didn't think he'd have much success. But he had never really considered asking for help in that matter, either. He was not the type to ask for help for anything. He had gotten this far on his own; he wasn't about to start asking for help at this time in his life.

As he thought about it now, though, there was considerable sense in the possibility that having the word of a sheriff and a Texas Ranger might go some way to helping him clear the path toward redeeming his name. But he couldn't be sure, and he was not about to risk his freedom. Not just yet, anyway. It was something to think about. Maybe one day not too far in the future, he would have Covington or McCracken test the waters up there to see what kind of reaction he might expect. He was tired of not being able to move freely about—except in Texas—because of the possibility of being arrested and imprisoned for some foolishness he had perpetrated more than a decade ago now.

Law pulled off his hat and wiped a shirtsleeve across his sweating forehead. It did little good, as the sleeve was soaked from the numerous times he had done this in the past hour.

For his part, McCracken peeled the sopping bandanna from around his neck and tried to mop the perspiration from his face, but with no success. "Damn, it's hotter'n a whorehouse on nickel night," he muttered. "I can't recall it ever bein' this bad."

Law could see no need to respond to that, so he didn't. Just kept riding, silently cursing the devilish heat that threatened to crush them as they moved slowly along across the prairie, the horses' hooves crunching on the dried grass.

After a couple of more hours of riding, though, the blazing, malevolent ball of the sun finally began to dip toward the far western horizon. It helped some, and the more it sank, the more the temperature slid. By the time McCracken pulled to a stop and looked around the countryside in the fast-fading sunlight, the temperature was almost bearable.

"We're gettin' close," McCracken announced.

"You sure?" Law asked. He was irritable after a long day in the furnace that west Texas was these days.

"Yes, I'm sure, goddammit," McCracken snapped back, no less annoyed.

They rode up a small rise and stopped at the top. Off in the distance, barely visible in the gray dusk, was a cluster of buildings.

"That's it," McCracken pronounced.

Law nodded, then surveyed the area to his left. He saw no one. He pointed, "Best ride on over thataway and swing around behind that barn from the west. But first," he added, "we best give these animals a breather." He dismounted and loosened the saddle on Toby.

McCracken did the same with his horse, and they stood, watching the darkness descend on them.

"What d'you figure to do once we get over there, J.T.?" McCracken asked. "I don't cotton to leavin' our horses out on the flats and sneakin' up on that barn."

"Me neither," Law commented. He would be damned before he left Toby—a horse that he considered of unequaled value—out loose where someone could just walk off with him. Not that he thought that anyone but him could approach Toby without spooking the animal anyway, but taking chances was not his way. Well, not taking foolish chances.

Law considered what to do, then decided within moments. "To hell with tryin' to hide, Jess. We'll just ride on in there, comin' up from the west side—away from the bunkhouses— and keep on goin' right into the damn thing."

"Bold as brass, just like always, eh?" McCracken said with a chuckle.

"Worked durin' the war, and it's worked for me these many years of huntin' down bad men; it ought to work here and now. It'll be dark, and I doubt anyone'll be payin' much mind to a couple of men just ridin' on in like they belong there. Most of them miscreants'll likely be in the bunkhouses anyway, gettin' likkered up or somethin'."

Law glanced at his friend, then grinned a little. "I reckon it would be a wise thing to take that damn badge of yours off, though. If we do run into anybody, that'd be a surefire way to put us in the middle of a battle we ain't got much chance of winnin'."

"That would be a troublesome thing," McCracken admitted as he pulled off the tin star and shoved it into one of his saddlebags.

"If we do encounter one of Kuykendall's men, we can just tell him we're new to the outfit. Just rode in from El Paso after Kuykendall wired us to come along to join the excitement."

McCracken nodded.

As the last of the day's light drifted off, the two men tightened the cinches on their saddles, mounted up, and rode off, moving slowly, uncertain of their path until the half-moon rose enough for them to be able to see a little better.

In little more than half an hour, they were riding through the wide doors of the barn. Two lanterns hanging from pegs in posts offered little light in the cavernous place. There was no one inside, though.

They dismounted. Law headed on foot toward the door,

saying over his shoulder, "I'll keep watch out here, while you pick out a couple of animals and saddle one of 'em. And don't go pickin' no crowbait, neither," he added, grinning, though McCracken could not see it.

Law stood just inside the door, leaning against the jamb, watching. He could hear McCracken behind him. He thought they were going to get away without ever being seen when two men started walking toward the barn.

CHAPTER 11

"JESS," LAW CALLED, voice little more than a hiss. He waved the lawman over, motioning McCracken to a position behind the door opposite where he stood.

When McCracken was in place, he peered around the corner and saw the two men coming toward them. Both were big, burly fellows dressed in rough clothes. Each had two pistols, worn high on their waists.

Law considered just giving them the tale he had concocted with McCracken, but something told him that wouldn't work. He glanced at McCracken. "We need to take these boys down," he whispered.

"Not tell 'em we're new here?" McCracken asked, surprised.

"I don't think these fellas'll believe it."

"Why not?"

"Instinct," Law said with a shrug. He couldn't explain it more than that, but he was sure McCracken would understand it. "No gunplay, though," he added. "That'll be sure to bring a heap of these miscreants runnin'"

McCracken nodded and looked around for something he could use as a weapon. Seeing the bulk of the two approaching men, he would need something to equalize the size disparity between him and either of the gunmen. He spotted a short-handled shovel leaning against the wall and grabbed it, dashing back to his spot by the door. He held it near the butt end as he waited behind the door.

Law flattened his back against the wall next to the door, almost grinning when he saw his friend wielding the shovel.

As the two men entered the barn, McCracken stepped up and swung the shovel at the one nearest him. But the man had just raised his arm to pick his nose, and the shovel, instead of mashing his face, bounced off his beefy forearm.

The man growled a little as he spun. Seeing McCracken with the shovel, his eyes widened in surprise and anger. Before the sheriff could swing the shovel again, the man stepped up, grabbed it, yanked it out of McCracken's hands, and flung it to the side. He moved in on the much smaller McCracken, taking a mighty swing at him with a cupped hand.

The sheriff was more nimble than the thug thought and managed to duck most of the blow, though what did catch him on the side of the head was still enough to knock him down. The man moved in on him.

At the sound of his companion getting hit with the shovel, the second man turned that way. He was about to go help his friend when Law stepped up behind him and, with hands locked together, pounded him hard on the back of the neck.

The man grunted and went down to one knee. "Sumbitch," he muttered, as he cranked his head around to see who had hit him. As he did, he started reaching for one of his pistols.

Law landed a roundhouse right to the man's face, cracking his cheekbone and the orbital bone around the left eye. The man groaned and swayed as he still knelt there.

Seeing the other man begin pummeling McCracken, who was doing all he could to both fight back and protect himself, Law slid a couple of steps to the side and kicked his foe under the chin. That broke the man's jaw and lifted him up and knocked him back, sprawling. He was barely conscious as he lay in the dirt moaning.

Law spun and ran the short distance to where the other big man seemed to be trying to pound the sheriff into the ground. Law grabbed him by the back of the shirt and jerked him back.

The man had better balance than Law had expected and remained on his feet. He lashed out, catching Law on the forehead with the back of his arm just above the elbow. Law staggered back a step, fighting to keep from falling.

The man swung a fist at Law, who managed to get an arm up and block most of it, though some of it got through, grazing his cheekbone and driving him back another step. The man swung the other fist, coming from down low, and it thumped into Law's gut. Though Law had been able to tighten his stomach in anticipation, staving off most of the damage, it still shoved him back a couple of more steps. The back of his boot caught on the other gunman's sprawled leg, and Law fell hard on his back.

The man swung around as he heard McCracken charging at him, and he grabbed the sheriff in a bear hug. He began squeezing the life out of McCracken, grinning viciously as he did so.

With a curse, Law scrambled up. He was about to pull one of his guns and just shoot the man when he remembered where he was and what trouble that would cause. He leaped forward and smashed the man on the ears with the outside of his fists as hard as he could manage.

The man yowled with pain and let go of McCracken, his hands going to his ears. Law grabbed him by the back of the shirt and the seat of his britches and, despite the man's size, spun him and ran him forward, then slammed him into a thick support post. The man's head bounced on the hard wood, and he sank to the ground.

Law turned to see the second man getting to his feet, trying once again to pull one of his pistols. Still not wanting to risk a gunshot, Law frantically searched the area with his eyes, then spotted a pitchfork near where McCracken was bent over, struggling to breathe.

Law swept the pitchfork into his hands and charged forward, driving the four thick tines into the gunman's chest with such power that they almost poked through the man's back, the only thing preventing that being the man's girth. The man fell, dead. But the movement jerked the pitchfork out of Law's hands.

The bounty man took a look around, assessing the situation with a practiced eye. No one else was coming, the one man was dead, and the other was out of commission for at least a few more minutes. And McCracken seemed to be recovering.

The sheriff looked at him and grinned ruefully. "Sorry, J.T.," he gasped, still having a hard time with his breathing.

"Nothin' to be sorry for," Law countered with a shrug. "You gonna be all right?"

"Yep. Any day now." He tried to smile, but it didn't work very well. He managed to straighten up, then nodded. "I'm all right. Just a tad short on air yet."

"Good. Go on back there and finish up with them horses. And get a wiggle on. We ain't got all night."

"What're you gonna be doin'?" McCracken asked as he drew in deep draughts of air.

"Takin' care of these two sons a bitches."

McCracken nodded and headed toward where he had been saddling one of the Kuykendall ranch horses.

Law went and yanked the pitchfork out of the man's body and tossed it aside for now. Then, sweating from the exertion, he dragged the corpse into an empty stall three-quarters of the way down the barn. That done, he walked back to where the other man lay. He was beginning to stir. Law had hoped the man would have died in the past few minutes, but that was not the case, and Law was not sure if the man would die now. With a shrug, knowing he could not allow the man to live— even if he was permanently damaged—because the risk was too great, Law reluctantly got the pitchfork again, stopping along the way to check outside. No one else was coming.

Then, steeling his heart, he walked over and thrust the implement into the man, killing him.

Law pulled the pitchfork out of the man and dropped it to the ground. Then he dragged that body to the same stall with the other one and left it there. Hurrying, he went back to the doors and checked outside again. Still no one coming. He picked up the pitchfork, which he brought to the stall. He used it to fork a pile of hay over the two bodies and then to spread fresh hay over the path along which he had dragged the bodies, covering up the trail of blood.

McCracken finished saddling the horse and had looped a rope around the neck of another. He led them, plus his horse and Toby, toward the door, where he waited for Law to finish his work.

Working fast, Law used more hay to cover up the blood where the two gunmen had died, then tossed the farm implement into the nearest stall.

He took a last look around, making sure things looked as normal as possible in the dimness, then nodded. He mounted Toby and held the reins and rope of the two stolen—recovered, he preferred to think of it—horses, while McCracken climbed into the saddle, then handed the reins and rope to McCracken. He would want his own hands free for battle, should that become necessary. They rode out of the barn and immediately swung to the west, moving away, taking their time, not wanting to attract attention.

Half a mile away, McCracken, who was in the lead because he knew the lay of the land better and because Law was watching their back trail in case of pursuit, turned them south. They rode slowly, though at a steady pace, wanting to make the best time they could under the circumstances. They had little reason to speak.

It was just after midnight when they pulled into the Drummonds' front yard, having come around from the south. It was a little farther because it was not as direct, but this way they were sure they had not been followed.

"Hello the house," McCracken called. "Luke. Luke Drummond!"

A lantern went on inside, but the front door did not open. Suddenly Drummond's voice came from the side of the house, "Who's there?"

"It's me, Jess. And John Thomas."

Carrying a rifle in his hands, Drummond moved away from the house. "Had to make sure, you know," he offered without apology.

"I would've thought you'd lost your reason if you hadn't taken precautions," McCracken said.

"You boys must be hungry," Drummond said, though it was basically a question.

"Reckon it wouldn't hurt to have a bite," Law said. "As long's Winnifred don't object none."

"She won't," Drummond said flatly. He moved up and shook the hands of both newcomers. "Even if she wasn't keen on the idea, knowin' it'd get Hank out of here all that much sooner would have her doin' it, and gladly, too."

"Speakin' of Hank, where is he?" Law asked as he dismounted.

"In the barn. I expect he's sleepin', though he might be awake worryin' about you boys for all I know."

Law nodded. "Well, if he ain't up already, he will be soon. Me and Jess need to see to these horses, and I expect me and Hank'll be pullin' out soon's we get fed."

"Don't you fret about the horses, J.T.," Drummond said. "They'll be taken care of." He yelled out, "Jasper, come on out here, son. You and Harold both." When nothing happened for a minute, he yelled louder. "You boys best get out here now!"

The door of the house opened, and the two boys hurried out. "We was gettin' dressed, Pa," Jasper noted.

Drummond nodded. "You boys take Uncle Jess's and Mr. Law's horses—and those other two animals—to the barn and make sure they're fed, watered, and curried well. They've been put to hard use and need proper tendin'."

"Yes, sir, Pa," Jasper and Harold echoed. They took reins and the rope to the four animals and led them away.

"If Mr. Blackstone's asleep," Drummond called after them, "rouse him up and tell him to get on over here to the house." He looked at Law and McCracken. "Let's go on in, boys," he added.

Inside, Law and McCracken sat at the table. Winnifred, surprisingly quiet, was bustling around the stove. Drummond hung the rifle on two pegs on the wall next to the door. Seeing it, Law shrugged, pulled off the shoulder holster, and hung it on another peg by the door.

"While Law did so, Drummond went to a cabinet, where he pulled out a jug. As he set the earthen container on the table, he grinned and said, "I bet you boys're drier than an old boot.""

"That we are, Luke, that we are," McCracken said.

Drummond got four glasses, set them on the table, and filled them with a goodly portion of the whiskey. "This was made from prime corn squeezin's," he said. "It ain't exactly what you'd find in some fine San Antonio or New York saloon, but it'll cut the dry in your throat."

Drummond decided not to wait for Blackstone. He held up his glass and said, "To the success of your endeavors, gentlemen."

The three clinked glasses and were taking their first sip when a sleepy-eyed Hank Blackstone entered. "I miss somethin'?" he asked grumpily.

"Just a small toast," Drummond said. "Come on, Hank, sit and have a snort of this fine bug juice."

Not long after they had downed their first glass of what was, in reality, pretty poor whiskey, a still subdued Winnifred dished up heaping portions of bacon and beans with sourdough biscuits on the side. Law and McCracken ate greedily, wolfing down the food with relish, sipping whiskey in between bites. Blackstone and Drummond ate with far less enthusiasm, having been asleep not that long ago.

While the men ate, Jasper and Harold returned, announced that the horses had been given better care than they probably had ever received before, and headed off to their beds. They had wanted to stay up and listen in on what their elders had to say, but both were too tired for it.

After the food, Drummond broke out some fat cigars. "Got these while I was in town," he said with a grin. "Knew enough not to get the kind you usually favor, J.T., so's no one would get suspicious. But I thought they'd be a fittin' way to finish off our last meal together."

"A fine way," Law agreed as he lit his cigar.

Winnifred served them all coffee, then put the large pot on the table. She kissed Drummond on the top of the head. "I'm off to bed, Luke," she said softly. She looked exhausted.

Drummond nodded and patted her hand, where it rested a

moment on his shoulder. When she left, Drummond asked, "So, did you boys have any trouble gettin' those horses tonight?"

"Depends on what you mean by trouble," Law said flatly. "We encountered a spot of difficulty, but not much."

McCracken shook his head, grinning at Law's underplaying their adventure. He explained what had happened.

When McCracken was done, Drummond whistled, impressed. "I'm glad to hear things weren't any worse."

Soon after, Law stabbed out his cigar on the tabletop and drained what was left of the coffee in his cup. He rose. "Well, Hank, it's time you and me were off."

"Now?" Blackstone was surprised. He had figured that since it was so late, Law would wait till morning before leaving.

"Yep. And I hope you like sleepin' out under the stars."

CHAPTER 12

✦

"WHAT'S THE RUSH, J.T.?" Drummond asked. "No reason that I can see for you to go leavin' in the middle of the night like this."

"Suppose some of Kuykendall's boys decided to follow us?" Law said not very convincingly.

"Ain't likely," McCracken offered. "And if they did, better you should be here to help fight them off, J.T., than off by yourself with just Hank, tryin' to take 'em all on—or, worse, havin' 'em show up here and me and Luke havin' to deal with 'em without your help." He had a sudden thought and cast a wide eyebrow at Law. "You would've already thought of that. So why're you really so all fired up to hightail it out of here?"

Law did not really know what to say. He just wanted to be away, though there was no real reason for it. "I thought Winnifred wanted Hank out of here," he said with a shrug.

"Well, sure she does," Drummond responded. He glanced over at Blackstone. "Not that she's got anything against you, Hank. It's just that, well . . ."

"I know," Blackstone said quietly, sadly. "Me bein' here is a danger to everyone."

"Yes, well, that can't be helped." Drummond looked back at Law. "Sure she'd like Hank to be gone; after all, it's pretty tryin' on her, as it would be for any woman. But a few more hours—when everyone's sleepin'—ain't gonna make any difference."

"I reckon," Law said doubtfully. He still could not explain his desire to be on the move, even after the long day and night he'd already had. It was just there.

"And if you stay," Drummond continued, ready with what he thought might be his most convincing argument, "you'll be assured of a fine, hearty breakfast to get you and Hank started on your way."

"That's a compellin' thought," Blackstone ventured. A vaguely eager look sprang into his eyes as he stared at Law.

The bounty man thought it over a few moments, then just as suddenly as he had decided to leave—and with as little reason—he changed his mind. He offered a smile. "I reckon one of Mrs. Drummond's breakfasts is a mighty compellin' reason," he allowed.

"That and the fact that a night's sleep—even if it is a short night—would do you well, eh, J.T.?" McCracken said with a grin.

"You're the one needs the sleep, old man," Law joshed. "'Specially after the whuppin' you took."

"I was just testin' you, boy," McCracken said with a chuckle. "Makin' sure you had the gumption to handle tough times."

"That's a steamin' pile of—" Law started.

"Well, you fellows can sit here and argue all the rest of the night, if you're of a mind to," Drummond said as he placed his palms on the table and pushed himself up. "But I am ready for some shut-eye." He turned and walked to the bedroom.

"I think Luke has the right idea," Blackstone said. He, too, rose and headed toward the door. McCracken and Law were right behind him, the latter grabbing his shoulder holster with the small Peacemaker from the peg near the door.

* * *

KNOWING THAT SHE would very soon be shed of Black-stone, Law, and McCracken, and have her household back, Winnifred went all out for breakfast in the morning. She was, as always, up before everyone else. She was quite busy at the stove by the time her husband had slumped out of the bed-room, still rubbing the sleep from his eyes.

"Wake Jasper and Harold," she ordered, though politely. "Then go rouse our visitors."

"Coffee first," Drummond croaked.

Winnifred handed him a tin mug full of hot, black coffee, which he gulped down surprisingly fast for all of its heat. He set the cup down, then woke the two older boys. In doing so, the oldest girl, Rachel, also woke. She hurried out to help her mother. The boys were slower to get moving. Drummond left them getting dressed as he headed out to the barn to get Law, McCracken, and Blackstone.

Law was up and brushing down Toby with long, gentle strokes. He turned when Drummond walked into the barn. "Mornin', Luke," he said with a short nod.

"Mornin', J.T. Winnifred says breakfast'll be ready right away."

Law nodded. While Drummond woke McCracken and Blackstone, Law gave Toby a couple of more swipes, then tossed the brush aside. He wiped his hands, grabbed the shoulder holster from where it hung on a post, and headed outside. The others followed moments later.

"Goddamn," McCracken snapped as he left the relative coolness of the barn. "It's gonna be another miserable hot day."

Law said nothing. He had already noted the temperature and could envision what riding through it for much of the day would be like. It was not an appealing thought. He sighed. There was nothing he could do about it, and there was plenti-ful and well-cooked food awaiting them. As he entered the house, the bounty man, as he had the night before, hung his shoulder holster on a peg near the door. He figured there was no need to have it sitting there in sight as they ate, especially with the children being around.

The men eagerly sat at the table, and Winnifred and Rachel began piling their plates high with food—slices of ham, hen's eggs, flapjacks, biscuits and gravy, butter, honey, jam, sausage, and coffee. Lots of coffee.

Afterward, almost groaning with the weight of the filling meal, the men took time for cigars—which Law passed around, thinking that he should have bought more at Wentworth's store—and another large mug of coffee each.

Finally, though, Drummond dropped his cigar into his coffee mug, where it died with a small hiss. "This's been fine, boys," he said, getting to his feet, "but it's long past time I was tendin' to my crops. You can stay here long as you want, but I got work to do." He had enjoyed himself considerably, but he had never stayed away from the fields for so long without a good reason. He was feeling a little guilty about it all.

"And I got to get back to Big Spring," McCracken tossed in, also rising.

"Reckon me and Hank best be on our way," Law offered. He glanced at Winnifred. "That was nigh about the finest feedin' I've had in many a day, Miz Drummond," he said with a smile. "You sure have a way with cookin'"

Winnifred blushed as she offered thanks for the compliments. She was rather flustered, not being used to such. She took pride in her cooking—and all her other wifely abilities—but it was far too often taken for granted. She would have to speak to her husband about that, and today, she decided.

The four men walked back to the barn—Law grabbing his second revolver as they left the house—where Drummond pulled back a canvas tarp covering the supplies he had bought yesterday, which rested in the back of his small wagon.

"You boys didn't think to ask for some things I thought you'd need," Drummond said. "So I took it on myself to get them for you."

"Like what?" McCracken asked.

"Rain slickers for J.T. and Hank, a bedroll for Hank, some eatin' gear for him, plus a frypan and boilin' pot, a coffeepot, and even a small Dutch oven—for biscuits and such, if you get a chance to make any." He shrugged. "I figured that J.T. travels light, so would only have small ones for just him. Extra lucifers and," he added with a grin, "a couple of bottles of bug juice. Strictly for medicinal purposes."

Law nodded and grinned. "You ain't so bad for a damn Yankee, Luke," he allowed.

Drummond laughed. "And you ain't so bad for a . . . friend of my old Rebel brother-in-law."

When the chuckling had faded, Drummond said, somewhat embarrassed, "I also took the liberty of buying each of you two boys a new shirt. I thought to send you off in style as much as we could."

"I'm obliged to you for your thoughtfulness, Luke," Law said. "It's mighty generous of you, but I'll be happy to pay for any of the extras."

"No, sir," Drummond insisted. "What the county don't pay for"—he cast a sharp glance at McCracken, but then winked—"and it should pay for everything, I'll pay for."

"I can't let you do that, Luke," Law said. "You ain't got the wherewithal to go payin' for fancies and extras for strangers."

"You ain't strangers," Drummond said firmly. "Besides, it's a small price to pay for makin' sure Howard County is rid of the likes of Chester Kuykendall, by God."

Law was about to protest some more, but McCracken cut him off. "Don't fret about it, J.T. The county'll pay for it all."

Law nodded and went to saddle Toby, while Blackstone saddled his new horse. McCracken and Drummond threw an old pack saddle on the other horse taken from Kuykendall and loaded most of the supplies on it. The rest of the supplies would go in saddlebags or—like Blackstone's bedroll—be attached to the saddle.

They all finished about the same time, but then had to take a few minutes to adjust the stirrups on Blackstone's saddle. While Law and Blackstone did so, McCracken spent a minute scribbling on a piece of paper, which he handed to Blackstone, who was sitting on his horse.

"What's this?" Blackstone asked.

"Bill of sale for the horse you're ridin' and the packhorse," McCracken said. "It ain't likely you'll get stopped by anyone, leastways no one official, but if you do, and they take note of the brand, you can show 'em that paper. It'll stand up to most scrutiny, though like I said, it's highly unlikely you'll need it." He offered a half smile. "I'd hate like hell to see you get hanged as a horse thief before you can testify against Kuy-kendall."

Blackstone looked like he was going to be sick for a minute. Then he gulped, nodded, and tucked the paper carefully into his shirt pocket.

Law mounted Toby. McCracken came up and held the bridle near the bit and looked up at the bounty man. "Judge'll be here a week from tomorrow," the sheriff said. "Best thing would be to get back into Big Spring early that mornin'."

Law nodded. "You take care of yourself, Jess. And don't forget those two boys I left in that mesquite thicket out there by the road way over yonder." He touched the brim of his hat in farewell and added, "Obliged for your hospitality, Luke. Tell the missus the same."

"I will do so, J.T.," Drummond replied. "God go with you both."

Law rode out of the barn, followed by Blackstone, who struggled with the rope to the packhorse. Since that animal was used to being ridden and not loaded down with supplies, it was not happy and was being rather uncooperative.

Law led the way south, across the prairie, farther from Big Spring and away from Kuykendall's ranch, heading for . . . Law had no idea where. He just figured to put some distance between Hank Blackstone and wherever Kuykendall's men might be looking for him. McCracken had warned him that Kuykendall had cowed many of the people in the area, who would think nothing of reporting that they had seen Black-stone if it would curry favor with the wild and dangerous Chester Kuykendall. Because of that, Law figured he would need to stay away from anywhere people might be—including the small farms that dotted the countryside at sparse intervals.

That had caused Law to wonder why McCracken would risk hiding Blackstone at the Drummonds' farm, even if for just a short time. He had even asked about it last night on the way to Kuykendall's ranch.

"Had no place else I could put him while I waited on you," McCracken had said. "Kuykendall doesn't have much to do with the farmers usually. They got nothin' he wants, really, though he'll deal with 'em when it suits his purposes. Like when they give him information that'll help him. And he'll intimidate 'em if he's lookin' for someone or somethin'."

"So why hasn't he tried to intimidate Luke?" Law asked.

"No reason to, I reckon. Far's I can tell, he don't know that me and Luke're related by marriage. I think he thinks Luke is just another small-time sodbuster. So he wouldn't send his boys out there to look around, since he has no reason to expect that Blackstone would be stayin' there."

The sheriff shrugged. "Like many arrogant men, he thinks he's smarter'n everybody else is. I think he thinks we have Hank stashed in Big Spring somewhere, hidin' him in the back of somebody's house or somethin'. Or he thinks we might've put him up in some hotel or somethin' in Mustang, off to the east of Big Spring, or Grayville to the northeast, or a dozen other small towns around the county. From word I've gotten from folks visitin' those places—and others—Kuykendall's men are makin' their presence known there these days."

"You got no help from folks there?" Law asked.

"Hell," McCracken said, drawing the word out in disgust. "I expect the town marshals in most of those places are, like Marshal Langenfeld in Big Spring, on Kuykendall's payroll. Or intimidated by him."

"Why hasn't he tried that with you?" Law asked. When McCracken cast an angry glance at him, Law added, "You know I ain't impugnin' your reputation, Jess. Ain't no man I know of more honest than you. But you got family—a wife and kids, even if he don't know about the Drummonds—and he seems like the kind of man wouldn't hesitate to grab up one of the young'uns and hold him to get you to do his biddin'."

"Shit," McCracken snorted. "That dog knows better. He knows I'd never abide somethin' like that. Oh, sure, I might do his biddin' for a spell, if he actually kidnapped Lucy Mae or any of the youngsters. But he knows that first chance I got, I'd put a bullet in his head and then kill every man jack who rode for him until I got my family back. He also knows that if he did take any of my family, and hurt them, I would hunt him—and every one of his goddamn men—down, no matter where they rode, and send them all to meet their maker."

"I'm surprised he ain't just had one of his men put a bullet in the back of your head and be shed of you and the trouble you bring him."

McCracken shrugged. "I'd be some surprised if he never gave it some thought. But, you know how these things go, J.T. Some folks get a reputation, and that intimidates even the baddest of the bad men sometimes." He offered an almost savage grin. "Just look at you. Your reputation as a hard case keeps a lot more men from comin' against you than it does makes 'em want to test their mettle against you."

"Reckon so," Law allowed. He never could figure that out. Some of the men he had hunted were heartless, cold-blooded, evil men. Yet his reputation had forced many of them to make mistakes they might not have made against a man with a less fearsome reputation.

CHAPTER 13

Hank Blackstone didn't know quite what to make of John Thomas Law. He rode along for much of the day, eyes focused on the bounty hunter's broad back. He was afraid of Law, yet at the same time glad to be under the bounty man's protection. He figured that if anyone could keep him safe until the trial, it was Law. Still, he wasn't entirely sure he could trust Law, not even with Sheriff McCracken's word that Law was a good man.

Law was certainly an intimidating man, what with his size, the deadly gleam that sometimes crept into those piercing blue green eyes, and those two deadly .45-caliber Colts he carried. It was enough to scare a fellow like himself to death, Blackstone thought.

Despite that, Blackstone was a little bothered by Law's silence. Law had seemed a gregarious enough man at the Drummonds' house, especially around the table. But out here, he had spoken not a word to Blackstone though they had been riding for several hours. Several times, he considered riding up alongside Law and trying to start a conversation.

But fear—and the fact that he didn't know what to say—kept him from doing so.

They stopped for a breather around noon out in the open—there was no shade to be found anywhere for miles. Law had been looking, hoping for something of an oasis to rest the animals. When he found nothing and saw that there was nothing even remotely possible on the horizon, he simply stopped where they were.

The heat pelted them mercilessly as they loosened the horses' saddles to let them breathe. Law wiped his drenched forehead with a soaking shirtsleeve. He got a canteen and drank deeply, then handed it to Blackstone, who gulped it.

"Pour some of that there water in my hat here," Law said when Blackstone was done drinking. "For the horses," Law said in annoyance when he saw the surprised look on Blackstone's face.

"Oh," Blackstone said, feeling stupid. He did as he was told.

Law let Toby drink all that was in his hat, then had Blackstone fill it again for his horse and then for the packhorse. Each man drank a little more, then Law capped the canteen and hung it back on the saddle horn.

"Goddamn, is it always this hot out here?" Law muttered. He pulled a bandanna from his pocket and wiped his face and head. Then he wrung the cloth out.

"Not usually this bad," Blackstone said quietly. "I think we're gonna git some rain, though, before too long, and that might help break this heat."

"Rain?" Law looked at the sky all around. There was not a cloud to be seen. "You must be *loco*."

Blackstone shrugged his round shoulders, dismissing his own comment.

"Don't be so shy, boy," Law snapped, the heat making him irritable. "You got somethin' to say, spit it out. I don't bite." He tried to grin but wasn't sure how successful he had been with it. "At least not too often. Or too hard." He couldn't help but chuckle at the look of horror on Blackstone's face. "Seriously, Hank, if you got something to say, you can say it. I'm here to keep you hale and hearty so you can testify against

Kuykendall. So I ain't about to go and hurt you just because you speak your mind."

"I don't want to ruffle your feathers, J.T.," Blackstone said, bravely using Law's initials. "You're doin' me a great service and . . . well . . ."

"Hell, boy, it's just a job to me. A job I think is necessary and one I take very seriously, but a job nonetheless. I ain't here to be your pa or your uncle or your pastor or anything else. I ain't the devil, boy, though there's some men who might make argument on that fact—if they was still alive." He chuckled a little.

"Yessir." Blackstone almost managed a smile. He sighed, then plunged on. "I've lived here all my life, and a man just learns things. Like tellin' when rain's a-comin'. I don't know how I know, but I know. You mind what I say—we'll have us rain within two days."

Law grinned to himself. "I'll take your word for it, boy." He paused, then said, "See, now that wasn't so hard, was it?"

"Reckon not." Blackstone relaxed a little. "I hope you and Sheriff McCracken weren't hurt too bad last night when you went and got this horse for me. And that packhorse. I'd hate to think you was stove up bad while tryin' to help me out."

Law grinned. "Hell, boy, I've been thumped a lot worse than that in a tussle in a saloon more times than I can count," he said. "Jess took the worst of this one, but even he wasn't hurt that bad."

When Law began to tighten his saddle, Blackstone hurried to do his own. As they worked, he said, "I wish I was as brave as you and Sheriff McCracken. Even half as brave. I'm just a nothin'. A dumb ol' farm boy who's afraid of his own shadow." He shook his head in self-disgust.

Law, who had been reaching for the stirrup, which he had looped over the saddle horn while he tightened the saddle on Toby, rested his hand on the stirrup and half-turned so he was facing Blackstone. "Now you listen to me here, boy," he said harshly. "I will not abide such talk from you. Just because you don't go out chasin' after bad men like me and Jess do doesn't mean you ain't brave. Me and Jess—and others like us—we just have a callin' to do what we do."

"But—"

Law overrode him. "But, you, you're the truly brave one here."

"How can you say that?" Blackstone asked, voice wobbling with emotion.

"Look at what you're doin', Hank. You're a man whose life is wrapped up in family and farmin' and leadin' a good and decent life, yet you're gonna bring an end to a man who has been terrorizing this county for years. That, friend, takes a heap of courage."

"Nah it don't. . . ."

"Like hell," Law said evenly. "How many times has someone testified against Kuykendall?"

"Well, never, but that's 'cause they all was killed before they could do so. Or so I heard."

"That's true. But despite knowin' that, you're still willin' to go into that court and tell the world what evil Kuykendall's been up to. That takes a heap more courage than most men got, even men who've fought in the war."

"Oh, I don't know . . ." Blackstone started, beginning to wonder if maybe Law was right. But that couldn't be, he told himself. He was just a farmer, not some kind of hero.

"Believe me, boy," Law said, as he plucked the stirrup off the saddle horn and let it drop to its normal position. "Pickin' up a gun don't make you brave. In fact, a lot of boys who've picked up a gun lookin' for courage have ended up dyin' needlessly. A brave man is one who takes on the bad men however he can—and that includes testifyin' in a courtroom against a man like Chester Kuykendall."

"I expect."

"Would you feel any braver if I gave you a gun?" Law suddenly asked.

"I reckon not," Blackstone said after a moment's thought. "I wouldn't know what to do with it. And," he added ruefully, "if I went and tried to use it against Kuykendall or one of his men to show 'em I wasn't afraid, I'd get myself shot to pieces."

"Yet you're going to walk into that courtroom and tell the people what Kuykendall done. That takes courage. And don't you doubt that." He pulled himself into the saddle.

Blackstone did the same, still looking ill at ease with himself. "More like hate," he muttered.

Law cranked his head around to look at Blackstone and stared a moment. "Never underestimate how much courage a good dose of hate can give you, Hank. If that makes you brave enough to do what you're doin', so be it. But it's also a decent and good thing to do. You don't do it, Kuykendall'll keep runnin' roughshod over this county. At least until someone like me comes in and sends him to the boneyard."

"That would make things simpler," Blackstone said with a harshness Law had not seen in him before.

"Might. But it might not be right either. Civilization's comin' to these parts, boy. And with it comes law enforcement. Real law enforcement. Not folks like me huntin' down bad men for money, but real lawmen protecting places."

"But I'm afraid, J.T." There, Blackstone thought, it was out in the open, and he was somewhat relieved that it was. Though he still had to live with the fact. "I'm even afraid of the hate I feel inside me for that man."

"Nothin' wrong with bein' afraid, boy," Law said. "If you weren't afraid, I'd be worried that you'd lost your reason." He clucked at Toby and rode off through the still smothering heat.

Blackstone trotted up alongside him. "You ever been afraid, J.T.?" he asked, worried that Law might get angry at the question, but he could not take it back now.

Law apparently didn't mind being asked. "Plenty of times, especially durin' the war. I don't know anybody who hasn't been afraid of somethin' at some time in his life. The problem ain't in bein' afraid, Hank, it's what you do with it. If you let it rule you, you won't live long enough for it to make a difference, like as not."

"Does it ever go away?"

"For some," Law said flatly.

"For you?"

Law chewed his lip as he thought that one over for a bit, trying to figure out how to explain it. Then he said quietly, "I reckon it has. When a man loses his fear of dyin', ain't much else can scare him."

"How'd that happen?" Blackstone asked, not realizing that

his fear of Law's possible reaction to his asking such personal questions had disappeared for the moment.

"When you lose about everything you loved or cared about and fall into the depths of despair, you don't much give a good goddamn if you live or die, so you're no longer afraid of dyin'." He didn't think it necessary to tell Blackstone that his depths of despair came at the bottom of too many whiskey bottles.

"Do you *want* to die?" Blackstone asked, excitement of a sort dawning on him. Or maybe it was something of a revelation. He didn't even notice that he was so caught up with what he had just heard that he was more outgoing than he had ever been; that the horrors of his recent life had faded, at least for the time being.

"Nope, I got no hankerin' to die, Hank. I just ain't afraid of it, so I can look it in the face without blinkin'. And," he added firmly, "I aim to do anything I can to prevent it from happenin'." He smiled grimly. "And I've gotten goddamn good at that."

Blackstone was going to ask more, but when he noticed the tight set of Law's jaw, he decided against it. But as he rode, he realized that he was no longer afraid. Of anything. Not even of dying. That, in fact, would almost be a relief. After all, everything that could have been taken from him had been. There was nothing left to lose, so nothing left to fear.

And as the fear left him, rage began seeping up inside of him to take the place of fear. It was a new feeling for Blackstone, and not an altogether unpleasant one.

LATE IN THE afternoon, Law came across a shallow wash that had some puddles from the last rain, whenever that had been. "This'll do for tonight, Hank," he said as he dismounted.

The two unsaddled their horses, then curried and hobbled the animals. "Go fetch us some bushwa," Law ordered as he began unloading the packhorse. By the time he was done, Blackstone had piled up a couple of armfuls of dried buffalo or cattle dung. Law knelt and got a fire going with the fragrant fuel and started some bacon, beans, and coffee cooking.

While they waited for the food to cook, Law and Blackstone took all three horses down into the wash to drink from the muddy puddles, then hobbled the horses and let them graze.

In due time, Law and Blackstone dug in, with some relish at first because they were hungry. But their enthusiasm waned rapidly.

"Sure ain't the same as Miz Drummond's cookin', is it?" Law said, fondly remembering this morning's meal. He did not look forward to another week of this.

"That's the Lord's truth," Blackstone said with a nod. "I didn't want to say anything, lest you think I was bad-mouthin' your cookin', J.T.," he added, trying to grin but not managing very well. He was still not capable of much in the way of joy or humor.

"From now on you can do all the cookin' while we're out here," Law said. Then he grinned. "Hell, I reckon we can take turns with it or somethin'. Your cookin' can't be no worse than mine, and it might be a damn sight better."

As was its nature, the buffalo chip fire burned hot but it didn't last, and not long after the two men had begun eating, it was almost out. "You want me to put more bushwa on there to keep the coffee hot, J.T.?" Blackstone asked.

"Nah. We'll save it for mornin'." Now that the sun had gone down, he wondered if perhaps it would be a good idea to have the fire going. Despite the day's sizzling heat, the night was going to be cool. But he decided that the fuel was too precious to waste just for the coffee. "Bushwa might be hard to come by before long," he commented.

"Why's that?"

"You seen any buffalo?" When Blackstone shook his head, he said, "Buffalo hunters pretty well killed 'em all off the last couple of years. Probably a good thing, I reckon. Once the buffalo was gone, the Comanches were a lot easier to run down and herd onto reservations. But they did make for some fine eatin'. And they were some sight to see." He shook his head. Everything was changing too fast. And not all the changes were to his liking, that was certain.

With a sigh of irritation for his sudden burst of sentimentality, he topped off his mug with the still-hot coffee, and with a nod indicated Blackstone should do the same. "It ain't gonna stay hot forever with the temperature dropping like it is," he noted.

Blackstone nodded and did so.

Law reached around to where his coat was still strapped to the saddle with his bedroll. He pulled it free and dug into an inside pocket, coming up with two cigars. He again wished he had bought more in Big Spring—or that Drummond had picked some up with the supplies. But neither had, so he would have to enjoy the few he had left. He handed one to Blackstone.

They leaned back against their saddles, puffing the cigars and sipping at the quickly cooling coffee. "So, Hank, how'd you come to be in this position?" Law asked, blowing a stream of smoke into the night sky.

CHAPTER 14

✶

"ME AND MY wife, Dora Jean, have—had—have, um . . ."
Blackstone sputtered to a stop, collected himself, and began
again. "I got me a farm over east of Mustang on Beals Creek.
Had us two young'uns, and was hopin' to start us a third soon."
He blushed at the intimate revelation.

Law suddenly didn't like where this was heading. He could
see nothing but tragedy arising from this story. But he said
nothing. Now that Blackstone had started, he would have to
continue telling it. Besides, Law thought he should hear it,
even if it wasn't pleasant, so he knew what he was really up
against with Chester Kuykendall and his small army.

"I went into town one day to run some errands." He could
still see the beginning of it as clear as when it happened,
though it was not that long ago—barely a month when he
thought about it. Later parts were still blurred by pain and an
unwillingness to accept what he had seen.

"I done purty much what I needed to and was gonna go to
a saloon to have a beer before headin' back home to Dora
Jean."

* * *

BLACKSTONE WAS WALKING past the bank when he heard a gunshot from inside. He leaned close, putting his face right up against the glass window, trying to see what was going on. When he realized that the bank was being robbed, he turned to run, figuring to shout an alarm as he was moving away from the place. He wanted no part of being caught in the middle of a bank robbery, especially one in which someone might have just been killed inside.

But the door burst open, and two men barreled out, crashing into him, sending him reeling. He instinctively reached out to grab one of the men simply to try to keep from falling. But all he succeeded in doing was to pull off the bandanna covering the bottom half of one man's face. Blackstone didn't know at the time that he had just encountered Chester Kuykendall. He found that out only later.

"You goddamn stupid puke," Kuykendall snarled. He was about to fire his pistol at Blackstone when two more men charged out of the bank, also slamming into the farmer, this time knocking him down.

Kuykendall and another man did fire then, but both bullets missed Blackstone, one plowing into the nearby hitching post, the other kicking up splinters from the wood sidewalk between Blackstone's chest and his partially outstretched arm.

Kuykendall, angry at having missed his target, was about to try to do the job right, but one of his men shouted, "Boss!" He pointed with his pistol.

Several armed townsmen were heading toward them, and others were taking up positions on roofs or behind water troughs. A few were beginning to fire at the outlaws.

"Dammit," Kuykendall snapped. "Get to the horses, boys!" He stared at the frightened Blackstone, as if memorizing his face. Then he pulled the bandanna back up so no one else would see his face, spun, and ran the few feet to his horse. He and his gang fled in a flurry of gunshots.

Moments later, men were helping Blackstone up. They led the dazed and confused man to the office of town Marshal Ike Endicott, where they sat him in a stiff-backed chair and handed him a shot of red-eye, which he downed without thinking. He choked a little, not being used to whiskey.

Finally Endicott shooed everyone out of his office besides his deputy and Blackstone. "You all right, mister?" the marshal asked solicitously.

"Yeah, I reckon so," Blackstone said, still dazed by all the confusion—and by having nearly been killed.

Endicott, an aging, slovenly, overweight man with a rapidly balding pate and some tobacco-stained, stubbly hairs on his upper lip that he tried to pass off as a mustache, looked at his deputy and said, "Smitty, give him another snort."

When Blackstone had drunk it—much more slowly this time—Endicott said, "Now, Hank—it is Hank, right? Hank Blackstone?" When Blackstone nodded, the marshal continued, "Now, Hank, tell me what happened."

Blackstone was surprised that Endicott looked a little worried, though the farmer decided it was only his imagination. He explained it, taking less than two minutes. Then he shrugged apologetically. "That's all there is, Marshal," he concluded. "I'm sorry I can't tell you any more."

"That's all right, Hank." He tried to hide his relief. "Do you know who the man was? The one whose mask you pulled off."

Blackstone shook his head. "Sorry, Marshal. Never saw him before."

"Would you know him again if you saw him?" Endicott's nervousness reappeared.

"I don't know, Marshal. Really I don't. It all happened so fast, and I was flummoxed when I was knocked down and all." He hesitated, wanting to be helpful. "I suppose I'd recognize him, if I come face-to-face with him again."

Endicott looked almost pained, but he recovered quickly. "All right, then, Mr. Blackstone, thank you for your help," he said in kindly tones. "If we need you for anything else, where can we find you?"

"Farm over on Beals Creek. Not far from town. You can't miss it."

"Thank you," Endicott said unctuously.

Blackstone left the office and walked down the street toward his mule, which was hitched to a rail outside the mercantile store. All thoughts of having a beer were long gone. All he wanted to do was go home and hug Dora Jean and their two children. He was shaken both by having been knocked down and by all the unaccustomed excitement. But by the time he had gotten home, he was practically back to his usual self and had a great time describing the incident to Dora Jean, who looked horrified by the fact that someone had shot at her beloved husband. He laughed at her womanly fear and told her how exciting it would be to testify at the trial when the bandits were caught.

"I don't understand you men at all," Dora Jean had said, still upset at having almost lost Blackstone. "Always seeing adventure in danger and such. It's enough to make an old woman out of me."

He hugged her close so she could not see the flicker of fear that had crossed his face at the remembrance of how close that one bullet had come to killing him.

Things on the small Blackstone farm went back to normal right away, and a week later, Blackstone rode his mule back into Mustang. Though he tried to tell himself he was not afraid, he gave the bank a wide berth. When he had finished his errands, he stopped by Endicott's office. "Have you caught those bank robbers yet, Marshal?" he asked.

"No," Endicott said testily.

"Well, I think I can remember what that man looks like," Blackstone said. "I could maybe describe him to you, kind of help you make a drawin' of him for a wanted poster or somethin'."

"No, Hank, that's not necessary," Endicott said hastily. "We got a description of him from other folks who got a real good look at him."

"All right, Marshal." Blackstone was feeling pretty good about himself and his willingness to do his civic duty. He had always thought himself a good citizen, but he had never really wanted to get involved in anything. But now it seemed right. "If you need my help in this, you just let me know."

"I sure will." When Blackstone stepped outside, Endicott turned and spoke to his deputy, who nodded and headed outside moments after Blackstone had.

* * *

BLACKSTONE WIPED SWEAT from his face as he plodded toward the house. It was just after noon, and he looked forward to a light meal and some time with Dora Jean and the children after a long morning of tending his corn and cotton.

Even from a hundred yards away or so, he suspected something was not right at the house. He stopped and looked carefully around. There was definitely something wrong. He could sense it, but he had no idea what it really was. There was just wrongness in the air. He began walking again, with long strides, but the uneasiness ate at him, and moments later, he began running.

The front door of the house was ajar, something that he took note of only in his subconscious as he burst into the house. He tripped and almost fell. As he righted himself, he turned to see what had caused his near spill, and the contents of his stomach erupted.

Four-year-old Emma Sue lay in a bloody heap near the door. When Blackstone finished vomiting, he scrabbled toward her on hands and knees and took her in his arms. Her throat had been slashed, and her front was covered with dried blood. Blackstone wondered where the salty wetness that suddenly touched his lips and dripped onto his daughter's face was coming from.

Blackstone finally set Emma Sue's body down. In a fog of numbness that precluded most conscious feeling, he rose and headed toward the curtained-off room at the back that the family used as a bedroom. He had planned to partition off a small room for Emma Sue herself soon.

Through eyes blurred with tears, he saw Dora Jean on the bed. She was naked and a god-awful bloody mess. Her throat, too, had been cut, and even though it sickened him no end, Blackstone was sure she had been raped. He stepped up and with a shaking hand slid her eyelids down, closing off the terror that lay in those green orbs.

He turned to the cradle alongside the wall to the left of the bed—Dora Jean's side. Lilly Ann, barely a year and a half old, was pinned to the bottom of her cradle by a Bowie knife through her stomach.

Blackstone managed to turn his head before he puked again, losing what little had been left in his stomach. Drained, he plopped down on the floor right there, heedless of the fact that he had almost sat in the mess he had made.

For how long he sat, he did not know. He had no sense of time, of reality, of anything. He was a vacant shell, a husk of a man. He was vaguely aware that darkness had sometime fallen, but he paid it no mind.

It was only when the cock crowed, and the new day's sunlight began to filter in even to the back of the house that he stirred. He moved like an automaton, with no real life in him. He wandered outside, managed to get a rope bridle on the mule, pulled himself on, and headed the animal in the direction of Mustang.

He stopped in front of the marshal's office, hardly aware that he had done so. He slid off the mule, almost falling. Carl Bockman, who was outside his hardware store setting up a display of tools for sale, saw him and hurried over.

"Hank, vhat's vrong?" Bockman asked, worried.

"Dead," Blackstone muttered. "All dead."

"Who? Who is dead?

"Dora Jean, Emma Sue, Lilly Ann. All of 'em. Killed. Cut to pieces."

A small crowd had begun to gather, the women horrified, the men trying to hide the same feeling.

"What the hell is goin' on out here?" Endicott asked, full of bluster as he emerged from his office next to Bockman's store.

"Hank says somevon killed his whole family, Marshal," Bockman explained.

"Well, bring him in," Endicott said. He seemed neither surprised nor in a hurry.

Bockman helped Blackstone inside and sat him down. "I better get him some food. He looks done in," the merchant said.

"Yeah, yeah. Good idea, Carl," Endicott said, dismissing him with a wave of the hand. He looked at Blackstone. "Tell me what happened."

"I don't know," Blackstone said. He shook his head, as if trying to clear out the horrible images imprinted on his brain. "I come home from the fields. At midday. Like always. Me and Dora always liked . . ." He shuddered. "They was . . . All of them . . ." Tears rolled down his cheeks, and great sobs racked him.

"How?" Endicott pressed.

It took Blackstone several minutes to answer. "Stabbed. Cut. Dora Jean was . . ."

"Yes?" Endicott seemed almost eager.

Before Blackstone could respond, Bockman returned with a plate of biscuits and gravy. He handed it to Blackstone. "Eat up," the merchant said. "You need your strength."

Blackstone took the knife and fork, put the plate on the edge of Endicott's desk, and began nibbling the food, not much interested in it but knowing he had to have something to eat.

Bockman looked over at Endicott. "Vas Hank able to tell you anytink?"

Endicott shrugged, annoyed at having been interrupted. "Bits and pieces." He sighed. "Trouble is, I can't help him none," he went on. "If they was killed out on the farm, it's out of my jurisdiction."

"But, Marshal, surely you can investigate sometink like this," Bockman said.

Endicott shook his head. "This is a problem for Sheriff McCracken." He did little to disguise his distaste at the name.

"Can you get him here?" Bockman asked, becoming exasperated. He could not understand Endicott's reluctance to be of any help in such a dreadful situation.

" 'Fraid not, Carl."

"Vhy you useless—"

"Watch what you say to me, boy," Endicott warned.

"Bah," Bockman snapped. "Come, Hank, ve vill get you some help vit' your family, and vit' havink somevon look into this." He glowered at Endicott.

Blackstone stood and let Bockman lead him out. He was still not functioning very well, and he was beginning to worry Bockman. The merchant took him to the funeral home, where they alerted the owner that they would have business soon.

"But you can't do anytink dere now, Herr Sanford. Ve must let Sheriff McCracken look tinks over first. Yah?"

Ed Sanford nodded. "I'll do what I can in the meanwhile." He looked at Bockman, then kind of nodded at Blackstone. "He going to be able to pay?" he asked.

Bockman glared. "Dot is a bad ting to ask at such a time," he snapped.

"Like any man, I expect to be paid for the work I do, Bockman," Sanford said.

"Vell, if he can't pay you for this, you thief, I vill," Bockman said before storming out with Blackstone in tow.

Bockman went to the livery, where he rented a horse and buggy. After making arrangements to have his son watch over the store for him, Bockman drove, with an inanimate Blackstone at his side, to Big Spring. He stopped in front of McCracken's office, helped Blackstone down, and they went inside.

"Ve—I mean Herr Blackstone here—needs your help, Sheriff," Bockman announced.

CHAPTER 15

✡

"YOU HAVE ANY notion of who might've done this, Mr. Blackstone?" McCracken asked when the story was mostly told.

"No, sir. Not really."

"Any notion of why?"

Blackstone shook his head. It was all still too horrible for him to really contemplate. He just wanted the images burned into his mind to vanish.

"Anything unusual happen recently that might've brought someone to do this evil?"

"Not that I can think of," Blackstone said. His voice was still defeated, lost, far off.

"Dere vas dot bank robbery," Bockman interjected. "It vas a veek, maybe ten days ago."

"Were you involved in that somehow, Mr. Blackstone?" McCracken asked. He was not too surprised, in a way, since he had, of course, heard of the robbery. In fact, he figured it was the work of Kuykendall's men.

"No," Blackstone responded, still dazed.

"You saw it, yah?" Bockman said, giving the farmer a nudge with his elbow. "Didn't you say dot?"

Blackstone looked at him, pain deep in his eyes. "Yeah, I did. I saw it." He turned back to McCracken, though he did not seem to be able to focus.

"Does anyone know you saw it?" McCracken asked.

"Sure," Blackstone said. "Lots of folks. And Marshal Endicott, of course."

"He even saw von of the robbers' faces," Bockman added, sounding almost as proud as if he had been the one.

"You saw one of the robbers?" McCracken asked, eyebrows shooting up. Now he was surprised.

Blackstone nodded. "Pulled the bandanna off by accident when he knocked into me."

"Do you know who it was?"

"Nah. Never saw him before." Blackstone sighed heavily.

"Maybe you better get over to Mustang soon, eh, Sheriff?" Bockman suggested.

"In a moment," McCracken said. "Can you describe this robber for me?" he asked Blackstone.

"Sort of tall, I guess. Thin, though wiry." Blackstone shook his head, trying to force himself to concentrate.

"Vhy do you vant to know dis?" Bockman demanded, worried about his friend.

"Maybe the robbers were responsible for what happened to Mr. Blackstone's family," McCracken said, with a glance at Bockman.

"Vhy vould dey—"

McCracken held up a hand, stopping Bockman. "Go on, Mr. Blackstone. You're doin' fine."

"He had a thin face, mighty pale," Blackstone said, fighting to concentrate. "Even paler'n mine. Red, frizzy hair and muttonchops that connected in a mustache."

McCracken cast a knowing glance at his deputy, who had sat quietly nearby all along. "You ever heard the name Chester Kuykendall, Mr. Blackstone?" the sheriff asked tightly.

"Nope," the young man answered after some thought. "Should I have?"

"Reckon not," McCracken said. He let out a large sigh. For

a few moments there, he had thought he might finally have something on Kuykendall that he could use to put the man away. But just as quickly, that hope had been dashed. "Have you talked to anyone about this?" he asked.

"Well, my wife. Dora . . ." His shoulders shook with emotion, and it took him some time to get himself under control.

McCracken waited him out, then asked, "Anyone else?"

"No, nobody," Blackstone said, voice ragged. "Well, nobody but Marshal Endicott. I told him just after the robbery that I seen one of the men who done it. I talked to him a couple days ago, too, when I was in town again. Told him I'd be willin' to describe the robber for him, maybe for a wanted poster or somethin'." He ran out of steam and came to a halt.

"Did he accept your offer?"

Blackstone shook his head.

That didn't sit well with McCracken, and he decided that he would have some hard questions for the Mustang marshal, whom he had long suspected of being in cahoots with Kuykendall. "When did you make that offer to him?"

Blackstone looked at the sheriff in a daze for some seconds. Finally he offered, "Two days ago."

That would, McCracken figured, give someone plenty of time to get from Mustang to the Kuykendall ranch and for Kuykendall—or more likely some of his men—to ride to the farm east of Mustang and kill Blackstone's family. Trouble was, he had not one iota of proof and little likelihood of getting any.

Still, McCracken vowed to himself that he would do everything in his power to find out who had done this horrendous thing and bring them to justice.

"Can you ride, boy?" McCracken asked Blackstone. He knew of young men who had lived their whole lives on the farm whose experience of riding was limited to bareback on a plodding mule or plow horse.

Blackstone nodded dully.

"Good." He looked at Blackstone's companion. "I'm obliged for all you've done for this young man, Mr. Bockman. I reckon we'll be needin' even more of your help before we get to the bottom of this devilment."

"I vill help all I can, Sheriff."

"Obliged." He paused. "Do you know if Mr. Blackstone here made arrangements for the interment of his family?" He spoke softly, not wanting to upset the farmer.

"Ve did—Hank und me. Before ve left Mustang to come here, ve talked to Herr Sanford. I told him not to do notink before you said is all right, though."

"That's good, Mr. Bockman. Now, why don't you head on home with that buggy of yours. Mr. Blackstone and I will be on horseback and will get to Mustang and Mr. Blackstone's farm long before you, I expect."

"Ya. I vill be at mine store if you need me for anytink," Bockman said with a sharp nod. He patted Blackstone on the shoulder. "Dis sheriff, he vill help you," he offered in soothing tones. "He is a goot man." He turned and left.

Moments later, McCracken and Blackstone walked out and headed to O'Fallon's Livery, where the sheriff had Sean O'Fallon saddle his horse and one for the farmer. Within twenty minutes of leaving the office, the two men were riding out of town. McCracken set a fairly good pace, hoping Blackstone would be able to handle it. But it was well into the afternoon by now, and the sheriff wanted to get to the farm before dark.

As they rode, McCracken went back over in his mind what Blackstone—and Bockman—had told him, trying to figure out how to prove that Kuykendall had done this, or ordered it done. But he slowly realized that doing so was going to be damn near impossible.

McCRACKEN DECIDED TO make a quick stop in Mustang. They halted outside the undertaker's. The sheriff considered leaving Blackstone outside but then decided that would subject him to the eyes and questions of the townsfolk. Blackstone didn't need that right now. "Light and tie, Mr. Blackstone," he said as he dismounted and wrapped the reins around a hitching post.

Still lifeless for the most part, Blackstone did as he was told and followed McCracken into the undertaker's.

"What can I do for you, Sheriff?" Ed Sanford asked

jovially when McCracken entered. His cheerfulness lessened considerably when he spotted Blackstone behind the lawman.

"We're headin' out to Mr. Blackstone's farm," McCracken said flatly. "I want you—or anybody you want to send—to head out there, too."

"Now?" Sanford asked, not looking forward to it. "It's edgin' up to dark, Sheriff."

"Yes, now," McCracken snapped.

"I'll have to have a portion of the cost up front," Sanford insisted. "In cash."

"Listen to me, you steamin' pile of horse droppin's," McCracken said harshly. "You'll be out there within an hour of my arrival there. If you're not, I'll be back here directly."

"But—"

"Even more, pard, you'll treat them bodies with the utmost respect and give 'em all the finest treatment and burial, or I swear you'll need your own goddamn services. You catch my drift, pard?"

Looking into the short man's blazing eyes, Sanford swallowed hard. "Yessir," he said.

"Good," McCracken said with a sharp nod. "And don't get your feathers all ruffled, pard. You'll get your goddamn money one way or the other." He turned. "Come on, Mr. Blackstone."

THE SCENE AT the house was every bit as horrible as Blackstone had described, McCracken found. As they approached the small sod home, McCracken had made Blackstone stay behind several yards from the front door. McCracken had gone on ahead, dismounting just feet from the door. While it was still light out, he wandered around the outside, examining the ground. He saw nothing of any real use, though there was one identifiable horseshoe print that might come in handy if he could match it with the horse it was on, which would be a formidable if not impossible task.

Finally he returned to the front door, glancing out at Blackstone, who sat on the horse like a statue, unmoving. McCracken steeled himself and went inside. It was dim inside the house, what with dusk rapidly approaching. He fired up a coal-oil lantern and looked around. He didn't need much light, really, to see the horrid scene. He could fully understand Blackstone's lack of animation. For such a young man, one who had never encountered violent death, coming into such a tableau would be enough to drive many men 'round the bend for all time.

He heard a wagon approaching, set the lantern down on the table inside, then walked outside just as Sanford and another man rode up. The back of the wagon contained three plain pine coffins—one regular size and two small ones.

"It's purty bad in there, boys," McCracken said as Sanford and his companion jumped down from the wagon.

"I've seen bad before," Sanford said stiffly.

McCracken shrugged. "Just remember what I said, pard, about treatin' them folks proper." He walked over to Blackstone. "You got any kinfolk in the area, Mr. Blackstone?" he asked. "Someone you could maybe stay with for a spell?"

Blackstone shook his head. "Parents died a few years back. Couple of sisters got married and moved off. Two brothers died in the fightin'."

McCracken nodded. He got his horse and pulled himself into the saddle. "Come on, Mr. Blackstone," he said.

Blackstone did not question, just followed McCracken back to town. They stopped in front of Bockman's store, dismounted, and went inside. "You been back long, Mr. Bockman?" McCracken asked.

"No. Just a few minutes is all."

"You know anyone who Mr. Blackstone could stay with for a few days?" the sheriff asked. "He says he's got no kin in the area, and judgin' by the way he's been actin', I don't think it'd be wise for him to be stayin' out at the farmhouse on his own."

"Yah, he can stay vit me and mein family," Bockman said without hesitation. "Ve vill vatch over him goot."

"I'm obliged." He turned toward the young man. "That all right with you, Mr. Blackstone?"

The farmer nodded, his faded blue eyes still showing few signs of life.

McCracken's heart went out to the young man. He could not imagine the pain Blackstone was going through, and he shuddered at the very thought of something like this happening to Lucy Mae and his children. He was suddenly filled with rage. "Don't you fret, Mr. Blackstone," he said through clenched teeth. "I aim to find the men who did this and make them pay, and pay hard."

Blackstone nodded again, but McCracken wasn't even sure he fully understood what had been said.

"Vhat vill you do now, Sheriff?" Bockman asked.

"I think it's time I had a little talk with Marshal Endicott." He walked out and next door to the marshal's office.

Ike Endicott was sitting at his desk shoveling food into his face. He glanced up, eyes widening. He swallowed hastily and pushed himself up, snatching the cloth bib out of his shirt collar. "Sheriff McCracken," he said, trying to hide his surprise—and the fear that had suddenly leaped into his stomach and chest. "What can I do for you?"

"Answer a few goddamn questions," McCracken said without preliminary or warmth.

"Sure. Whatever I can." He waved a hand vaguely at the plates on his desk. "You want a bite while we talk?"

McCracken ignored the question. "What've you done about the killin's of Mr. Blackstone's family?" he demanded.

"Well, nothin', really." He swallowed hard, uncomfortable with the sheriff's iciness and the line of questioning. "Like I told Hank, it's out of my jurisdiction. So I sent him to you."

"That's a yellow-hearted attitude," McCracken practically spat. "Have you done anything about the robbery here a couple of weeks ago?"

"Not too much." Endicott's attempt at looking nonchalant failed by a wide margin. "I got nothin' to really go on."

"Mr. Blackstone told me—and others," McCracken said pointedly, "that he saw one of the robbers and was willin' to describe him so you could get a wanted poster out on him."

"Yeah, well, that's true, I reckon," Endicott said, shuffling nervously. "But you know how people can be. I ain't so sure he really did see anyone. And if he did, I ain't so sure he got a good enough look at him to make it worthwhile."

McCracken was about to tell him that Blackstone had given him a fine description of the robber but then decided

against it. He was certain that the marshal was in Kuykendall's pocket, and to give him too much information could
be fatal to Blackstone. "You should've at least tried," he finally said.

"Maybe you're right, Sheriff," Endicott allowed, sounding
almost apologetic. "We don't usually have such doin's here,
so I ain't used to checkin' these things out."

"Then maybe Mustang ought to have a different marshal."
He paused, realizing he could do little more here. He had deep
suspicions about Endicott, but he could prove nothing there
either. "You best hope," he finally said, "that nothin' bad happens to Mr. Blackstone. Or it'll be your ass, boy." He turned
and stormed out of the office, knowing that if he didn't leave
immediately, there was the strong likelihood that he would
shoot the marshal down.

CHAPTER 16

✶

WITH THE HELP of Carl Bockman, Hank Blackstone pulled himself together to some degree in time for the burials of Dora Jean, Emma Sue, and Lilly Ann two days later. Afterward, Bockman had Blackstone to supper at his house and insisted that the farmer spend another night with the family. The next morning, Bockman drove the young man home.

"You vill be all right here by yourself?" he asked, worried.

"I reckon so, Carl. I'm much obliged for all you and your family've done for me since . . . since . . ." He choked back more tears.

"Ya," Bockman said sadly. "Vell, Hank, you take care of yourself. If you need anytink, you come see me."

"I will, Carl, thanks." With heavy steps, he headed into the eerily quiet and frighteningly empty house. And, without much enthusiasm, he rose the next morning, made himself breakfast after a fashion, then headed out to tend to his crops, which had been much neglected these past few days. He was working under the blistering sun for a couple of hours when he saw a rider approaching.

He stopped what he was doing and pulled off his old hat and wiped his head with a bandanna, watching the rider get closer and closer. Fright bit deep into him. He could see no reason for anyone to come riding out here to see him, unless it meant trouble. He tried to tell himself it was likely Sheriff McCracken, or maybe even that useless town marshal, Ike Endicott, coming to talk to him about the robbery he had witnessed.

He was quite surprised when his cousin, Curly Adams, pulled up on his horse and dismounted. Adams had changed considerably since the last time Blackstone had seen him eight years or so ago. Adams was taller and leaner than Blackstone remembered, whipcord-tough looking. He wore black pants and expensive black boots, a collarless calico shirt of white and green stripes under a brown leather vest. Around his neck was a large bandanna with the bottom point hanging near the bottom rib of his left side. A tanned, hard face peered out from under a costly Stetson. And he wore two ivory-handled revolvers.

"Whatcha doin' here, Curly?" Blackstone asked, shaking his cousin's hand, nervous at the tough look Adams wore—and the two pistols.

"Come to see you, Hank," Adams said flatly. "I hear you been gettin' cozy with the sheriff over in Big Spring."

"Just went to tell him about my fa . . . fa . . . family." He was close to tears again.

"I heard about them," Adams said dryly.

"Why would someone do somethin' like that?" Blackstone wondered aloud, the shock of it still strong in him.

"To send a message, boy," Adams said harshly.

"A message? What kind of message?" He shook his head. "What the hell are you talkin' about, Curly?"

"You been flappin' your gums an awful lot about that bank robbery, boy. It was unfortunate you saw what you saw there. If only you had forgotten about it, things might've been different."

"What's that mean, Curly?" Blackstone asked, gaining a little courage. This was his cousin, after all, not some stranger, even if he was well heeled.

"It means you should've kept your mouth shut about that robbery. There's some men don't like folks who talk too much."

"The man I saw at the bank that day did this?" Blackstone

asked. Shock, disgust, rage, and fear fought for supremacy inside him.

"'Course not," Adams said unctuously.

Blackstone didn't believe him, but the look in Adams's eyes scared him enough not to question it. Instead, he asked, "So what'd you want to talk to me about, Curly?"

"Didn't say I wanted to talk to you, boy," Adams said flatly. "Tell you true, I was sent here to kill you."

"What?" Blackstone exploded. He dropped his hoe. He might have taken off running, but he was too frightened to move. "Why?"

"Look, Hank," Adams said, softening a little, "there's big doin's goin' on in Howard County. The man I work for has big plans, and he expects to be runnin' things hereabouts before much longer. I'm his top hand, so I stand to be a big man 'round here, too. But we can't have folks talkin' to the law about some things. Now, Mr. Kuyk—I mean, my boss hoped you'd take the hint when he sent boys over here to . . . send you a message a couple of days ago. Instead, you went and talked to Sheriff McCracken. That wasn't smart, cousin."

"How was I supposed to know that was a message?" Blackstone snapped, forgetting for the moment his fear as his anger grew. "All I knew was that I come home from the fields and my wife and my fam . . . everybody . . ." He stopped, sucking in a jagged breath. "What was I supposed to do? Somebody had just butchered my family."

Adams shrugged. "All I know is that when Mr. K—the boss heard you was talking with Sheriff McCracken—who went to talk to Marshal Endicott, raising questions that are alarmin' to the boss—he ordered me and a bunch of the boys to come kill you."

"Where's the others?" Blackstone asked, blinking in fear.

"Didn't bring 'em. When I heard it was you he wanted killed, I talked him into lettin' me go it alone. Don't ask me how; I just did. And, being his trusted top hand, he allowed it."

"And?" Blackstone asked, fear almost overwhelming him.

"And, I ain't gonna do it," Adams said flatly. "It's why I wanted to come here alone. I owe you, boy."

"Owe me?"

"You remember that time you pulled me from that pond after Dick Clayton hit me in the head with that rock?"

"Sure, I remember." They were ten or eleven years old when their friend Dick Clayton, who was on the smallish side, got angry at something Adams had said. He picked up a rock and pitched it hard at Adams, hitting him in the head, and knocking him into a deep pond. Blackstone had jumped in and fished his cousin out, then pumped his lungs until Adams spat up a heap of water.

"You kept me from drownin', cousin. I would've been dead for certain, hadn't been for you. So now I'm payin' you back. Instead of killin' you like I'm supposed to, I'm gonna give you some advice—get the hell out of Howard County. Get as far away as you can get, and then stay there."

"What'll I do?" Blackstone wondered, flummoxed by all that he had just heard.

"Farm, boy, that's what you do. Find a new gal and start yourself a new family. You're young."

"Supposin' I stay in these parts?" Blackstone asked. He might be frightened, but he did have a stubborn streak in him.

"It'll be your death, cousin," Adams said bluntly. "And mine, too, if the boss finds out that I didn't kill you like I was supposed to. The boss ain't a very forgivin' man."

"Reckon I got no choice, then," Blackstone said fatalistically. He didn't know how many gunmen Adams's boss had at his command, but even if it were just Adams, it was more than Blackstone could handle. He was no fighter.

"That's bein' smart, Hank." Adams turned and placed a hand on the saddle horn, ready to pull himself up, then stopped and looked back. "I am sorry about your family, cousin. They really wasn't supposed to go that far. They was just supposed to put a scare into 'em. Well, into your wife, so's she'd get you to shut your trap. But those dumb bastards . . ." He shook his head. Adams was a man used to violence and killing, but he could not abide something like this. It was repulsive. But it was too late for him to change it now.

"Curly," Blackstone said quietly, as Adams mounted the horse. When Adams looked at him, the farmer asked, "Who was it who sent those men here the other day?"

"I can't tell you that, Hank," Adams said flatly.

"God almighty, Curly, I got a right to know, especially if I'm gonna leave here and never even be able to visit their graves again."

Adams sat there on his horse for more than two full minutes, just staring out across the plains. Then he said, "Chester Kuykendall." He jerked the reins around and heeled the horse into movement. "Now get your ass out of Howard County, cousin," he shouted over his shoulder as he rode off.

Blackstone let that sink in for a moment. It was the same name Sheriff McCracken had mentioned to him the other day. He wondered what would possess a man to do what this Kuykendall apparently had done here—and elsewhere, if the sheriff knew of him. But there was no answer, he supposed, as he bent and picked up his hoe. Some men were, he guessed, just pure evil.

He went back to work as his mind continued to work over the information he had just received. But he had no choice. He would have to leave here. His breath caught in his throat as he realized that it was bad enough he would never see Dora Jean, Emma Sue, and Lilly Ann again, but it was crushing to know he would never even be able to visit their final resting place.

As the afternoon began to fade, he dropped the hoe, figuring he would not need it again, and he trudged back to the house.

IN THE MORNING, Blackstone packed whatever foodstuffs and personal items as he could in burlap sacks. He loaded them on the mule. He went back inside for one last look. There was so much he had to leave behind since he had only the mule. One of the axles of his wagon was broken, and he had no time to fix it. Not that he would have cared anyway. The effort would have been too great in his despair, and his fear that Adams, or worse, some other of Kuykendall's men, would return had him eager to get away. But it was still very hard.

With a great sigh, he turned and, taking the rope he had tied around the old mule's neck, walked away from the house, each step both easier and more difficult. He walked east, following Beals Creek, plodding along in no hurry. Several times he felt as if he were being watched. He stopped at those times and looked around, but he never saw anyone. It only increased his fear, even though he tried to tell himself the feeling was his imagination. Or, if real, it was probably just Curly Adams keeping an eye on him, making sure he did leave the county.

Fear and anger vied for dominance as he walked for the next couple of days, but slowly anger began to win out, and soon had all but wiped out the fear. The more he thought about it, the more he wanted revenge for the murders of his wife and two young daughters. He knew he could do nothing himself, not being a gunman, but he realized he could testify against this Kuykendall and his gang of killers, however many of them there were. It didn't matter to him that he really had little to testify about against any of them, except perhaps Kuykendall himself, but it didn't matter. He trusted in the sense of justice of his fellow Texans.

Four days out, and not having had the feeling that he was being watched for a day, he turned southwest. He walked a little faster, his step more assured, as he told himself with every mile that he was not afraid, that he was going to get the men who had killed his family.

About midday three days later, he came to the well-defined road heading northwest to Big Spring. He neared the town a couple of days later but stopped at a mesquite thicket to wait. It was late afternoon, but he did not want to be seen coming into town. As darkness began to fall, he started walking again. Under the cover of night, he marched into town and straight to Sheriff McCracken's office.

Fear again swept over him, but he fought it down, trying to think clearly. He decided that it might not be wise to leave his mule out front of the office, even in the dark, so he went to Third Street and down that to an alley that ran behind the sheriff's office. There he tied the mule, patted it a few times on the head, then walked back out to Main Street and the office.

A surprised McCracken listened intently to everything Blackstone had to say, then nodded. When Blackstone was finished, the sheriff asked, "And you'll testify in court to all you just told me?"

"Yessir." It was strange. Blackstone had thought that once

he had come this far, he would not be frightened any longer, but the fear was back inside of him, stronger than ever.

McCracken made arrangements to keep Blackstone hidden for a few days, but he knew he could not do so forever and perform his regular duties, too, especially after he arrested Kuykendall, which he planned to do as soon as he could. He had a deputy take Blackstone's mule to the livery, telling O'Fallon that the animal might have been stolen and that the sheriff was checking it out. He put Blackstone up in a cell for the night, swearing his deputies to silence. And he sat there wondering what to do about Blackstone until the judge could arrive. While sitting at his desk, pondering the situation, he glanced over at the wall—and the stack of wanted posters stuck there with a small knife. He smiled, thinking he had his answer.

The next morning, McCracken sent wires to several places where he thought John Thomas Law might be, and waited anxiously for an answer. Fortunately, he had one by shortly after noon.

With Blackstone safely ensconced in the jail for the time being, behind the wood wall that would keep him out of sight of anyone visiting the office, McCracken wondered what to do with him.

Moments later, Luke Drummond popped in. When he saw McCracken's drawn face, he asked, "What's wrong, Jess?"

McCracken explained.

"Ah, hell, he can stay at my place for a few days," Drummond said. "Till this fellow Law gets here."

"Winnifred ain't gonna allow that."

"I'll talk to her," Drummond said with confidence.

Just after dark, the two rode out with Blackstone covered up in the back of Drummond's wagon. They left him sitting outside while they went inside to talk to Winnifred. She had, of course, refused to have anything to do with having Blackstone staying there, and she voiced her opinion loudly and often.

Finally, however, Drummond had hushed her. "No one's gonna think to look here, Winnifred," he said. "And Jess says this professional fellow will be here in a couple of days. We can let this fellow stay here that long."

"It's a danger to our family, Luke," Winnifred insisted. "And we don't know what kind of feller he is."

"He's a farmer, just like you and Luke," McCracken said, his patience stretched thin.

"Besides, Winnifred," Drummond said, "it's the right thing to do. If it will help put this Kuykendall away forever—and protect this whole county in the doin'—then it's worth a bit of risk."

Winnifred argued some more, until Drummond finally said, "Enough, Winnifred." He looked at McCracken and nodded.

CHAPTER 17

J.T. LAW WAS stunned at the story. He had been through some damn hard times in his life, but he had never even come close to the personal tragedy that Hank Blackstone had. "Goddamn, boy," he said quietly. "You're a hell of a lot braver than I was givin' you credit for in plannin' to testify against Kuykendall. Hell, with what you been through, most men'd be a thousand miles from here by now."

Blackstone managed a wan smile. "Thanks," he said.

"So Marshal Endicott really was in cahoots with Kuykendall?" Law asked after several minutes of silence.

"I reckon so," Blackstone answered. "Sheriff McCracken and I finally figured that after I went to the marshal and offered to describe the robber—that bastard Kuykendall—for a wanted poster, he must've sent someone out to find Kuykendall and tell him that I knew too much. Or he thought I knew too much." Blackstone shook his head in amazement and anger. "Hell, I didn't know Kuykendall from the president at the time. At least not to put a name and face together. So Jess figures Marshal Endicott told Kuykendall, who sent those men who . . ." He fought back a sob. "Dammit, dammit, dammit," Blackstone snapped. "If I hadn't tried to be so helpful, I probably wouldn't be in this pickle and Dora Jean and the young'uns would be . . ."

"You were tryin' to do the right thing, boy," Law said. "You can't blame yourself for what happened to your family. Endicott is a skunk and a devil for associatin' with that bastard Kuykendall. He's just as guilty as Kuykendall is. And once Kuykendall is safely tucked away in prison or danglin' at the end of a rope, Endicott will answer for his transgressions, one way or another," Law added grimly. "I promise you that."

Blackstone nodded. He slid down into his bedroll. Reliving the story had exhausted him. "G'night, J.T.," he muttered. He was asleep in moments, though his slumber was beset by a variety of demons.

THE NEXT DAY, they turned vaguely southeast. Law wasn't sure where to go. In almost any direction was danger. Big Spring was, of course, out of the question. Southwest of the town, though a fair piece northwest of where they were now, sat Kuykendall's Double Bar K ranch. Back behind them was the Drummonds'. East of Big Spring was Mustang—and Blackstone's farm. In between, the prairie here on the edge of the Llano Estacado was dotted with other towns, farms, and some ranches. Law didn't think Kuykendall had many friends or relatives in the area, but he would not be shy about using intimidation—or even cash, considering that most of the farmers were barely scraping out a living here in this rugged land—to get information from people. So Law and Blackstone would have to avoid anyplace with people around, which could make the next week or so mighty interesting.

Finally pushing that problem out of his mind for the time being, Law began wondering about other things.

Like why Kuykendall would have personally helped rob a bank, especially some piddling little bank like the one in Mustang. McCracken had said that Kuykendall apparently rarely went on these criminal rampages, preferring to leave it to his henchmen. There could be, Law figured after a while, a number of reasons why he had done so. Men like Kuykendall would get itchy after a while, and he might have just felt like getting some action, especially since Mustang was way over to the east of Big Spring, where he wouldn't be very well known, it being well away from his ranch. Or it could be, Law reckoned, that his men might be getting restless and irritable because they were doing all the work, taking all the risks, and he was getting the money, so Kuykendall put himself on the line to show his men he was still capable of it. And it would have been smart to pick a small town and small bank, so the danger would be minimal. Of course, it could be something simple, such as McCracken being mistaken, and that Kuykendall took part in more crimes than McCracken thought, leading by example. Men like Kuykendall often craved action, and someone who had raised such a large and hard organization in such a short time would be as arrogant as hell. Or maybe Kuykendall just plain had a personal vendetta against the bank owner or the town for some real or imagined slight.

Law finally shook his head to clear it. None of this had any importance to him. And it didn't really matter why Kuykendall had been arrogant enough—or stupid enough—to have taken part in robbing that bank. As it turned out, it was going to be his downfall.

Spotting a farm in the distance, Law turned north. Blackstone followed silently, seemingly not paying much attention to where he was or where he was heading. He still wrestled with his grief and fear and rage, each in turn taking the upper hand, only to be overcome by one of the other emotions, and on and on.

The day darkened as they rode, with swarming clots of black clouds gathering. Law and Blackstone pulled out their slickers and kept them handy. About an hour before what would have been dusk, the skies opened up. Law growled as he pulled on his slicker.

He glanced back at Blackstone, who tried again to grin. He was getting minutely better at it, Law thought, but he still had a long, long way to go before he got any actual humor or pleasure in the smile.

"Told you, J.T.," Blackstone offered.

Law grimaced and turned his face back toward the front. He soon stopped at a clump of shin oak, declaring that they had come far enough for the day. The brush provided no shelter from the rain, but it did give them enough fuel to manage—after several attempts—a small fire under one of the larger bushes that served to heat coffee for them.

"The rain's good, J.T.," Blackstone said as they chewed on leathery jerky and sipped coffee that rapidly cooled in the air that had grown chilly.

"Sounds like somethin' a farmer would say," Law groused. But he was grateful for the rain in that it pooled in many spots, giving the animals plenty to drink, and it would be easy to fill their canteens. Still, he didn't much care for it, especially since it meant pretty much a cold camp.

It was still raining steadily, and showing no signs of letup, when they rode off in the morning. By afternoon, Law was sick of it. He turned in his saddle, water dripping off his fancy, flat-crowned hat. "This goddamn rain ever gonna end?" he asked.

"Sooner or later," Blackstone responded with forced joviality.

Sometime that night the rain finally did start to slow, and by morning it was over, though they still could not get a decent fire going, Law's spirits did rise a bit as they moved off for the day. With the end of the rain, however, came the return of the heat.

In late morning, Law spotted some riders in the distance and veered off to the west. They traveled slowly, in no rush, since they had no place to be. The following day, Law turned them north again, and they crossed the main road between Big Spring and San Angelo.

"We're getting mighty close to Mustang," Blackstone said in the late afternoon. The fear had returned in force. He did not want to be anywhere in the vicinity of Mustang, where so many people knew him. The whole idea of his being with Law was to keep him hidden—and safe—until the trial. He didn't think being within a few miles of Mustang was all that safe.

Law nodded. He knew they were somewhere in the vicinity

of the town, but he didn't know how close. "We'll stop soon," he said. "There any decent places to spend the night?"

"Stand of mesquite about half a mile that way," Blackstone responded, pointing.

"How far is it from town?"

"Two miles, give or take a little."

"Good," Law commented.

"That's too close," Blackstone said, trying to control the renewed fear.

Law stopped, letting Blackstone catch up with him. "We'll be all right, Hank," Law said quietly. "Don't go lettin' the fear get the better of you again. You're too strong and brave for that."

Blackstone sucked in a long breath, then let it out slowly. "I'll be fine, J.T. Let's go."

They started riding again, this time side by side. "This stand of mesquite, is it big?" Law asked.

"Pretty good size. Why?"

"We should have enough wood for a decent fire," Law said. "And that means a decent meal." He paused, almost smiling. "Well, as decent a meal as the two of us can concoct."

The stand of gnarly trees was, indeed, of fairly good size, and a decent amount of the fragrant-burning wood was lying around for the taking. They built up a good fire, and Blackstone cooked up a Mexican dish of beans and spices and, for the first time since they had left the Drummond farm, a batch of biscuits in the small Dutch oven.

When they had finished, Law rolled a cigarette. He offered the pouch of tobacco to Blackstone, who shook his head. He pulled out his corncob pipe, filled it with some of his almost depleted supply of tobacco. He fired it up. Both men relaxed, leaning back with their smokes and a cup of coffee. They were silent, each with his own thoughts.

Blackstone thought that this was almost pleasant. If not for the reason he was here—the murder of his family—he would enjoy this. The food had been edible, if not near the quality made by either Dora Jean or Winnifred Drummond, the coffee was thick and properly bitter, the biscuits light and fluffy, his pipe comforting.

Still, he could not help but think that this would be close to paradise if Dora Jean was sitting across the fire from him instead of John Thomas Law. He still could not fully comprehend that she was gone, that she and their two daughters had been so brutally massacred. He wished more than anything that he could see them again. Tears crept into his eyes, and he was thankful that in the dark Law could not see them.

Law flicked his cigarette butt into the fire, drained his coffee, and put the tin cup down. "Reckon it's time for some shuteye," he said. With a yawn, he stretched out on his bedroll; it was still too hot to really want to wrap in the blankets.

Blackstone nodded. "G'night," he said, voice again filled with pain and despair. He knocked the ashes out of his pipe and lay down on his own bedroll. As he drifted off to sleep, visions of Dora Jean lingered in his mind, taunting, haunting him.

Sometime not long after midnight, judging by the moon, Blackstone awoke with a start. He lay there on his blankets, heart pounding, unsure of what had woken him, his mind a jumbled confusion of images and desires. He got up, still uneasy, and headed off behind one of the mesquite trees and began to urinate.

As he was standing there going, it came to him in a flash. He almost splattered himself in his excitement before he put himself away and buttoned up his trousers. Heart still racing, he turned and walked as silently as he could to his horse—he considered the animal his now, by dint of use and possession. He slipped the bit into the horse's mouth and the bridle over its head. He stood there a minute, trying to decide whether to saddle the mount, too, then decided against it.

Taking the reins in his hand, he walked the horse away from the camp. A hundred yards away, he stopped. Realizing he was not going to be able to just leap up onto the horse's back, he looked around in the moonlight, then walked on a little more, still searching. Finally he found a fairly large rock. He brought the horse up to it, then stood on the rock to mount the horse bareback.

Settling on, he got the horse moving, his body tense with a combination of exhilaration, expectation, and fear.

* * *

WHEN LAW AWOKE, he lay there for a couple of minutes, listening to the sounds of the world around him. Everything seemed normal at first. Then he became aware that something was missing. He cranked his head around and noticed that Blackstone's bedroll was empty. He nodded. That was what had been wrong, he decided; he had not heard Blackstone snoring. He figured the farmer had risen to go relieve himself. Which, Law decided, was not a bad idea.

He rose and stretched, then took two steps toward a tree, and stopped short. "Where the hell is his horse?" he muttered. He stayed where he was, head rotating on his neck, taking in everything. Toby was there, placidly munching grass, as was the packhorse. The supplies were still piled neatly off to one side. His bridle hung from a mesquite branch. Blackstone's saddle, which he, like Law, had used as a pillow, still rested where it had been the night before, as did the farmer's bedroll.

The only explanation was that Blackstone had taken off on his own; he had not been forced to leave. The big question was why. Had he gotten too frightened and decided to run? That could be, though why he would have done so leaving his saddle, bedroll, and supplies behind? Unless he was just so panicked that he had wanted to get as far away from here as fast as he could, not wanting to take the time to saddle the horse and gather up what supplies he could carry.

Law battled down the rush of anger and confusion. He walked to where Blackstone's horse had been, then managed to find the tracks of it leading out of the camp. He followed it far enough to find the rock Blackstone had used to help get on the horse. He followed the tracks a little farther, but decided that Blackstone had not appeared to be running the horse, so he probably was not in a hurry to leave. It only made it all the more mysterious.

With growing annoyance, Law headed back to camp. He relieved himself, then stoked up the fire and got coffee going, then began making breakfast—more bacon and beans, which didn't make him happy, but he needed something fast and filling. It was likely to be a long day ahead, and he would need his energy.

He ate quickly and dawdled only long enough to gulp down a second cup of coffee and smoke half a cigarette. Then he hastily, haphazardly cleaned the pots and plates before loading the pack animal. He finished that and was just beginning to saddle Toby when he heard something.

Yanking out the larger Colt from the hip holster, he slipped behind a couple of mesquite trees and watched. "I'll be damned," he muttered as he saw Blackstone riding calmly toward the camp. Even more startling was that the young man looked more at peace than he had since Law had met him.

Law slid the pistol away and walked toward the oncoming Blackstone. "Where the hell've you been, goddammit?" Law demanded when Blackstone was a few yards away.

CHAPTER 18

✡

FEAR LEAPED BACK into Blackstone's eyes as he slid off the horse. "Went to see their graves," he mumbled, head low.

"What? Whose graves?" Law asked. He was so angry he wasn't thinking straight. Then it dawned on him. "The family?" he questioned. "You went to see the graves of your wife and children?" He was incredulous.

Blackstone nodded, still unwilling to meet Law's gaze.

"You goddamn fool," Law snapped. "You were the one so worried about being this close to Mustang in the first place. What the hell ever possessed you to go and do such a damfool thing?"

"I don't know," Blackstone muttered. "I woke up in the middle of the night, and just . . . well, I just had to go and do it. It's almost like somethin' was pushin' me to go." He shrugged his drooping shoulders, unable to explain it any better.

"You could've been seen, boy," Law growled. "Too many people in that town know you, and you know Kuykendall's got to have some people around there who are loyal to him or would want to get on his good side."

"It was dark," Blackstone said defensively.

"It ain't dark now." Law only hoped that no one had been around to see Blackstone at the cemetery. But nothing could be done about it now, one way or the other. He sighed, calming himself. It would do neither of them any good for him to stand here and berate the young man. What was done was done.

"All right," the bounty man finally said. "Go and saddle up that horse." He squinted at Blackstone for a moment. "You didn't abuse that horse by ridin' him too hard, did you?"

"No, sir. Took my time."

"Well, that's good," Law grudgingly acknowledged. "So go saddle him up. You're gonna have to do without food, at least till we stop for a noon meal—if I decide we will stop. Everything's been put up, and I'll be ready to ride soon's I saddle Toby."

Blackstone nodded. Despite Law's annoyance and the possible danger, which he really didn't think was that great, he felt good about having visited the graves of Dora Jean, Emma Sue, and Lilly Ann. It had served to temper the fear a little more, and increase the anger, but in an odd way—it was a slow, simmering fury that burned deep and steady inside of him, steeling him for what lay ahead.

Law wasn't much given to worrying about things he couldn't change, so as he saddled and bridled Toby, he let his annoyance settle down. Considering what Blackstone had been through, Law couldn't fault him too much for wanting to visit the graves when they were so close. Law did, however, curse himself for having brought them so near to Mustang. He had been riding mostly aimlessly, just trying to avoid any place with people, using up the time until the trial. He should have paid more attention yesterday when Blackstone had told him they were so close to the town and backtracked a ways or changed direction. But that, too, could not be changed.

They mounted their horses and rode off, Law heading due east, away from Mustang and Blackstone's farm to the north. As he plodded along, Law looked for some kind of shelter where he and Blackstone could hole up for a few days. In some ways that might make them more vulnerable, since they would not be on the move. On the other hand, this constant traveling across the open prairie was not particularly safe either. It was too easy to be seen, and if they did encounter any of Kuykendall's men, defense would be a problem.

About midmorning, they had to veer south for a bit when they spotted a small shack in the distance. Law considered checking it out and possibly using it, but as he studied the rickety structure from a distance through his telescope, he saw a couple of people moving about. So he moved on, keeping well away from them—and later in the day, from the herd of cattle they caught sight of.

"It's gettin' a mite crowded round these parts," Law commented in irritation as they turned north, away from the herd of longhorns. They soon skirted the ranch house, then turned back to the east.

Late in the afternoon, Law looked over at Blackstone, riding alongside. "You gettin' a tad tired of bacon and beans, boy?" he asked.

"Reckon I could fancy somethin' different," the young man allowed. "You got somethin' in mind?" He almost grinned. "Like maybe some beefsteak?" He pointed back the way they had come, where the herd of cattle was now several miles behind them.

"You want to be a rustler?" Law joshed.

"Well, not really." Blackstone paused. "It ain't like I really dislike ranchers, but such folks do cause problems for us farmers a powerful lot of the time. Killin' a longhorn on the sly to fill my belly wouldn't bother me much."

Law grinned. "Reckon it wouldn't me either were I in your shoes, boy. But they're a far piece back, and I ain't turnin' around just so's you can settle some small score with a rancher you never met."

"What do you have in mind?"

Law pointed.

"Deer or antelope?" Blackstone asked, squinting to make out the small group of animals a few hundred yards ahead near a spreading clump of redberry juniper.

"Does it matter?"

"Reckon not. I've et both, and both're tasty feedin'," Blackstone allowed.

"My thinkin', too." He pulled out his telescope and extended it, then peered through it. "They're deer, though."

"Venison sounds good."

As they rode slowly toward the herd, Law began to wonder if perhaps his hunger—or, rather, his desire for something new for supper—wasn't overriding his reason. Firing a shot or two might draw some attention, if there was anyone within hearing distance. But they had seen no one since the cowpoke or two by that shack. They hadn't even seen anyone with the cattle, though he assumed there were some cow punchers somewhere in that vicinity, but that was at least five miles back by now. He decided it would be safe enough.

They rode until they were about a hundred yards from the deer, several of whom picked their heads up and looked around nervously. Law and Blackstone stopped and dismounted. Law handed Toby's reins to Blackstone. He pulled his Winchester from the saddle scabbard.

"Be back directly," he said before moving off toward the deer. While he was a good enough shot with a rifle, his ability with the long arm was nowhere near that of his talent with a revolver. So he wanted to get as close as he could before firing. While one shot might not be too dangerous, two or three very well might be. He was determined to have some venison, but he was equally determined not to fire more than one round.

At about forty yards, the deer started getting restive, and Law stopped. He dropped to one knee, levered a round into the chamber, and brought the rifle up. He was more used to firing the weapon from horseback in the midst of battle, so this, as always, felt a little odd to him. But he settled in, took his time aiming, then squeezed off a shot. One of the deer jumped, ran several steps, and then fell. The rest of the herd bolted, bounding off in great loping, bouncing strides.

Law rose and waved Blackstone forward. While he stood there waiting, he scanned the horizon all around, watching to see if the gunshot had attracted anyone. But by the time Blackstone reached him, he had seen no one.

"You know how to butcher a deer, don't you, Hank?" Law asked.

"Reckon so. I've butchered pigs and chickens and helped my pa some years ago butcher a deer."

"Then have at it," Law ordered. As Blackstone moved off toward the dead deer, with his horse and the packhorse in tow, Law stayed where he was. He mounted Toby to get more height and therefore a better vantage point. He continued his lookout while Blackstone did the butchering.

When he saw that Blackstone seemed to be nearly done, Law rode toward him but swung a little to the side and out another fifty yards or so. Then he rode back. "Looks like this'll do for tonight," Law announced. "There's little bits of standin' water round the other side of this juniper. Ain't much, but it'll allow the horses to drink some, which they need. We'll set up camp round there, too."

"Beals Creek ain't but a half mile or so north of here," Blackstone said, wiping his hands off on the outside of the deer skin.

Suddenly remembering his charge's venture the other night, Law asked, "Your farm's on Beals Creek, ain't it?"

"Yep."

"How far from here?"

Blackstone stood for a moment looking around, getting a fix on where they were. "Eight, ten miles, maybe a bit more," he finally said.

Law nodded. That should be far enough to keep Blackstone from making another dangerous and foolish journey. "All right. Load some of that meat on the packhorse, boy," he ordered.

They were soon on their way, and not long after, crossed the creek to get to the small stand of cottonwoods on the north bank. Law dismounted and tied Toby to a tree branch. "I'll take care of the horses—and keep a watch out—while you fetch up wood and get a fire going," he said.

"THIS WAS A good idea you had, J.T.," Blackstone said an hour later as he chewed on a succulent piece of roasted venison.

"Reckon it was," Law allowed. So pleased was he at having something other than bacon and beans, that he ended up eating considerably more than he normally would. He knew that would likely mean extra time in the bushes come morning, but it would be worth it.

After eating, Law sat back with a cigarette and Blackstone with his pipe. Law pulled his watch from his pocket and clicked it open. He stared at it, apparently oblivious to the world around him.

Blackstone saw the gold watch flicker in the low light of the small fire. This was not the first time Law had gazed at the watch, and while Blackstone could not be certain because of the darkness, he suspected there was a longing in Law's eyes whenever he did so. "That watch must be mighty special," he said very softly.

Law jerked out of his reverie. "It is," he said tightly, snapping the watch shut.

"Sorry," Blackstone said, even more curious now. He knew there was a picture in there, and he wondered who it was.

"It's all right."

"An old sweetheart?" the farmer asked.

"That's none of your goddamn affair," Law snapped, the pain of loss rising up inside of him. Then he remembered what Blackstone had gone through so very recently, which made his own loss insignificant by comparison. "Sara Jane Woodall," he said more contritely.

"What happened to her?" Blackstone asked, his own tragedy squeezing his heart.

Law smiled sadly. "Nothin' *happened* to her, Hank. She just threw me over."

"Why would she do that?" Blackstone asked. He figured any woman would find John Thomas Law a fine catch, not like the poor farmer that he himself was.

"Her folks and mine took opposite sides when the fightin' began. After the war, there was still bad blood, though my folks were dead, and she still wouldn't have anything to do with me. I wasn't very conciliatory toward her because of some things her pa had done either." He fought back the anger. It was a long time ago, and he was annoyed that it still irritated him so much. He should be over all that by now, he figured.

"He sighed. "Can't say as I blame her, I reckon. I don't think I would've made a very good farmer or even rancher." He offered another sad smile. "I did love that gal, though," he added.

Law slid the watch back into his vest pocket and slid down on his bedroll. "'Night, Hank," he said, pulling his hat down over his eyes.

"THAT'S THE OLD Pederson place, I think," Blackstone said.

He and Law sat on their horses atop a low rise. The bounty man peered through his telescope at the farmstead a couple hundred yards away.

"Don't know what happened to 'em," Blackstone added. "I thought they was still about, but it sure don't look it from here."

Law snapped the looking glass closed. "No, it don't." He thought a moment, then asked, "How far is it to Big Spring?"

"I ain't sure, but if I remember from hearing the Pedersons talk about it one time, it can't be more than four, five miles."

Law nodded. "Stay here while I go take a look around." He edged Toby forward, eyes scanning the horizon, the house, and the area all around. There was nothing that would indicate there were people around. He rode past two large cottonwoods that shaded a slightly tilting outhouse. What had been a garden patch lay fallow to one side of the house. An old chicken coop had collapsed.

As he neared the sod house, Law could see that part of the roof had fallen in and the door was barely hanging by one leather hinge that would not last much longer. The bounty man dismounted and stepped inside. A few pieces of old furniture were scattered around, but that was about it. He went back outside and waved at Blackstone.

"Reckon this'll do till we got to go back to Big Spring," Law said when the young man arrived and stepped down off the horse.

Blackstone was relieved. He was plumb tired of all the riding. It was not something he was used to, and after nearly a week his rump was mighty sore.

They unloaded the supplies, which were getting thin, tended

the animals, and then settled in. They kept the three horses inside with them for much of the time. It meant hauling in grass and other forage at times, but it was better than having the animals outside where they could be seen by anyone passing by. Fortunately, the pump near the house still worked, so they had plenty of fresh water, and they took the horses out at least twice a day to let them drink from the trough and move around a bit.

The next two days passed quickly and uneventfully. On their third afternoon there, Law said, "We'd best get an early start in the mornin', Hank. Don't want to keep that judge waitin'."

The two were sitting at the table. Law was just starting to reload the smaller of his two Colts after cleaning it, having done the larger one a little while ago.

Blackstone, who was half dozing, jolted awake. "Suits me," he said. "I want to get this over with."

"You still all right about testifyin' against Kuykendall?"

Blackstone nodded. "Damn right I am." He paused, then admitted, "I'm still scared to my bones, but I want that bastard to pay for what he done to Dora Jean and the children." He rose, stretched, and yawned. "Reckon I'll go pay a visit to the small house out there." Still yawning, he headed out through the now-doorless entryway.

Moments later, the sharp crack of a gunshot split the hot afternoon air.

CHAPTER 19

JOHN THOMAS LAW snapped the loading gate of the small Peacemaker closed and thumbed the hammer back. With the weapon in hand, he darted toward the door, flattening himself against the sod wall just to the side of the opening. He peered around the jamb.

"Goddamn son of a bitch," he muttered when he saw Blackstone lying sprawled in the dirt halfway between the house and the latrine. The young man was not moving.

He thought he could see the last of a puff of gunsmoke drifting away from a slight hillock almost two hundred yards away, though he could not be sure. Still, it seemed a likely place for someone to have been to fire a shot at Blackstone.

Law almost called out to see if the farmer was still alive but decided against it. He didn't know if whoever was out there knew that Blackstone was not alone here, and he did not want to give away his presence unnecessarily. Besides, from the way it looked, there was little chance that Blackstone was alive.

The bounty man stayed there for some minutes, waiting to

see if someone was coming toward him. When he was fairly certain no one was going to rush him just yet, he slid the Colt into the shoulder holster and turned back inside. He went to his saddlebags and got out a box of cartridges. While he had seen no one coming, he fully expected an attack at any moment, and he was going to be ready. Whoever it was out there was going to be in for one nasty surprise if he expected to just walk in here.

He opened the box of bullets and put it on the table and went back to his post by the door, staring out, watching, but still saw no one coming. Turning away, he grabbed what was left of a small stool that he and Blackstone hadn't gotten around to burning for a cook fire yet. He went to the back corner of the house, shoving the horses out of the way, and stood on a rickety chair. He used the stool to pound on the back wall where the roof had fallen in. Since there were no windows or doors in the back, he wanted a way to be able to watch for an attack from that direction.

He was sweating heavily from the exertion within a minute, but it did not take long before he had knocked out a section of sod, giving him a good view of the back and much of one side. Someone could still sneak up on the other side of the house, but there was nothing he could do about that now.

Wiping his face on a bandanna, he went back to the side of the door and watched for a while. Then he went to the back, where he had opened up the wall, and watched.

Throughout the tense, sweltering afternoon, he alternated keeping guard at the two places. As the day wore on, he grew more surprised that no one had attacked him. He couldn't understand it. It was hard enough to believe that someone had found them—or, more precisely, had found Hank Blackstone—but it was impossible to understand why they would have killed the farmer and then let Law alone. Unless, Law thought sometime during the day, they did not know Blackstone and Law were together. That seemed even more preposterous. If they had tracked down Blackstone, they would have had to have known he was with Law.

The bounty man finally decided that whoever was out there was either waiting for him to show himself, at which time they would shoot him down the way they had Blackstone, or they were going to wait until dark and then move on the house and kill him then.

Or try to. Law was not about to let either happen. He had been in a lot tighter spots than this and had gone against men a lot smarter and tougher than this bunch.

As the day began to fade, Law started to prepare. He saddled Toby and Blackstone's horse and put his saddlebags and bedroll on Toby. He returned the box of cartridges for the Peacemakers back into the saddlebags. He tied a rope around the packhorse's neck, then cut some short lengths of rope. He made periodic checks of back and front as he worked. When everything was as ready as he could make it, he waited, face grim.

As soon as full dark had fallen, and before the moon had really risen, Law slipped outside. Rushing to Blackstone, he grabbed the young man's body and slung it up over his shoulder, then hurried back inside the house.

Hating to do it, but knowing it was necessary, he flopped Blackstone's corpse across the saddle on the farmer's horse and swiftly tied it down, using the lengths of rope he had cut earlier. With the sun down, the temperature had slid, and it was getting cool, so he slipped on his black frock coat, Then he led the three horses outside.

Law swung up onto Toby's back, took the reins to Blackstone's horse and the rope on the unburdened pack animal, and rode off. He moved slowly, trying to make as little noise as possible so he would not give himself away nor cover up sounds others might make.

Half a mile away, he picked up the pace, breaking into a trot. He wanted to distance himself from the farmhouse as quickly as possible. He just hoped Toby did not hit a chuck hole or something.

The moon soon rose, shedding a thin, silvery light over the landscape, giving it an eerie look. The moon was both a relief and a potential danger for Law. On the one hand, he could see where he was going somewhat, thus being able to take an easier course. On the other hand, if he could see, anyone who might be following him could see, too, meaning he could be spotted. And, while he was not afraid of a face-to-face confrontation, even against heavy odds, he could do nothing about someone taking a rifle shot at him from a distance.

He did not worry about that, really, because he could do nothing to prevent it. He simply acknowledged that it was a possibility and let it go at that. And he kept up the pace, face set in a mask of grim determination.

Law finally slowed when he spotted a smudge of light on the horizon. He avoided all the roads into Big Spring and approached across the plains, passing O'Fallon's Livery, and up to Third Street, where he turned into the pitch black of the alley that ran behind the sheriff's office. He stopped roughly where he thought the back of the office was.

He dismounted and, after groping around for a few minutes, found a hitching rail to which he tied the three horses. Then he marched to Third Street, out to Main Street, around the corner, and into the office.

A deputy sat at the desk. His eyes widened when he saw the bounty man. "What can I do for you, Mr. Law?" he asked.

"Where's Jess?" Law asked flatly.

"Havin' some supper down to the Llano House restaurant. He usually goes home, but he sent the family off to visit kin somewhere, what with the judge comin' into town tomorrow sometime." The deputy made an exaggerated search with his eyes. "Where's Mr. . . . um, the witness?"

But Law was already walking through the door. He strode up the street, his size and demeanor making what few people were out and about step aside.

Jesse McCracken looked up when Law stepped inside the restaurant and stopped. The sheriff froze, coffee cup halfway to his mouth, and his face drained of blood when he saw the look on Law's countenance. McCracken set the cup down, stood, and tore off the napkin that had been tucked into the collar of his shirt. He grabbed his hat from the table, said something to a waiter, and hurried to Law.

"What the hell's gone on, J.T.?" he asked, worried.

"Tell you outside." When they were on the street, Law said, "Somebody got Hank."

"What?" McCracken asked, eyes round. "How? Where?"

"This might not be the place for it."

"You're right. Let's go to the office."

In silence they hurried down the street. When they got into the office, McCracken said, "Go do your rounds, Charlie."

"But, Jess, there's no rounds—"

"Then go have a beer or something. Anything," McCracken snapped. "Just go."

When the deputy had left, looking angry and confused, McCracken perched his behind on the edge of the desk.

Law spun a straight-backed chair around and sat on it, forearms across the top of the back. "We found us an old farmhouse four, five miles north of here," the bounty man said flatly. "Hank said it was the old Pederson place."

McCracken nodded. "I know it."

"We spent three days there. This afternoon, Hank went outside to visit the shitter, and somebody put a bullet in him from a couple hundred yards off, best I can figure. I figured if they got him, they'd be comin' for me, too, so I hunkered down. But nothin' happened. Soon as it got dark, I got Hank's body on a horse and got here fast as I could."

"Je-sus," McCracken muttered. "Not that it matters, I guess," he asked after a few moments, "but how'd they find you two?"

"I ain't sure they knew I was there. If they did, why didn't they come gunnin' for me?"

McCracken shrugged. This was too much for him at the moment. "Then how'd they find Hank?"

"I ain't sure of that either." He had given this some thought on the ride here this night and had come up with only one possible explanation. "But what I think happened is someone over in Mustang saw him a few days ago."

"Mustang? How? When?" He shut up, knowing he was gibbering.

"We spent most of our time since leavin' Luke's wanderin', tryin' to keep out of sight. One night, we ended up fairly close to Mustang, without me really knowin' it till it was too late. We should've kept movin', goin' off in another direction, but I figured we were far enough from the town—Hank said it was a couple miles—to be all right. But that goddamn fool slipped out of our camp durin' the night and went to visit his family's graves."

McCracken groaned.

"Only thing I can figure is that someone saw him, even though he said it was still dark when he left there, and somehow got word back to Kuykendall. Then Kuykendall sent his men out to scour the county." He thought about it. "I guess some of his men must've known the Pederson place was supposed to be empty, and they either came by to check or were just passing by when they saw some smoke from our fire. Or maybe they just saw some other indication that the place was being used, and waited."

"When did he make this little excursion to the cemetery?" McCracken asked after almost two full minutes of contemplation.

"Five nights ago. Why?"

"Three days ago, a guy we think is—or was—Kuykendall's top hand turned up dead just here in Big Spring."

Law shrugged. "So?"

"His name was Curly Adams."

"Never heard of—" He stopped. "Wait, that's Hank's cousin, ain't it? The one who warned him to get out of Howard County?"

McCracken nodded. "Yep. And shortly after that warning, Hank came to me to offer to testify."

"How'd he die? During a robbery or somethin'? A gunfight?"

"He was hanged by the neck from a rafter at O'Fallon's. Had a note pinned to him that said, 'This is what happens to traitors.' What I think happened was that he told Kuykendall he had killed Hank like he was supposed to, figurin' that his cousin would hightail it and no one would be the wiser. But then somebody must've seen Hank at that graveyard and got word to Kuykendall, who realized that Adams had let Hank go. So he had Adams killed and then sent his men out to find Hank and kill him."

Law thought that over for a bit. It all made sense and would explain a lot. "You know," he said slowly, still thinking it through, "I don't think Kuykendall knows I'm involved in this. If your theory is right about Hank and this Adams fella, whoever saw Hawk probably saw him alone. When Kuykendall's men killed him, they must have figured he was alone, which is why they never attacked me."

"Seems right." McCracken paused. "So where's Hank now?"

"Out back. About the same place, I reckon, Hank left his mule when he came here to offer to testify." The self-disgust at having failed in his job flooded over him again.

McCracken could see it in his friend and knew it boded ill for somebody. He had to get the bounty man's mind off things for now. "We've got to take care of Hank," he said.

Law considered shoving past McCracken and going straight back to the cells there and killing Kuykendall. But he knew the sheriff was bound—by duty and by honor—to try to stop him. Law knew he would have no trouble taking Jess McCracken, but he was not about to kill a friend over the likes of Chester Kuykendall. No, Kuykendall could wait. He would pay, that was certain, but now was not the time.

"All right," Law said.

Taking a lantern, they walked around back, got the horses, and walked with them to the Trigueras brothers' undertakers. McCracken pounded on the door until Pedro, who obviously had hastily tied his tie and slipped on his jacket, opened the front door.

"He gets the best," McCracken said as two of Trigueras's workers carried Blackstone's body inside through the front; McCracken had refused to go around the back for it.

"*Sí*, of course," Trigueras said.

"Send the bill to the county. He's to be buried over in Mustang, next to his wife and children."

"It will be done, *Señor Alguacil*—Sheriff."

McCracken walked back to his office, and Law rode to the livery, where he turned over all three horses for caring. Then he went and got himself a room in the Llano House and ate in the attached restaurant. Then he went to Wentworth's store and pounded on the door until Alva Wentworth, who lived in the back, opened up. He was not happy about doing so until he realized it was Law. He greeted the bounty man warmly.

Law picked up a couple of new shirts, pairs of pants, and a frock coat, and a handful of the small cigars he favored. Wentworth charged him less than he was owed, but Law didn't have the energy to argue. He just said his thanks, got the name of a seamstress, and left. He had to wake the woman, but when he promised her three times what she usually charged for alterations, she agreed to take his clothes and work on them right away. Law finally got to bed.

After a light breakfast and several cups of coffee in the morning, Law went to the seamstress's house and picked up his clothes. Back at the hotel, he put on a new shirt, trousers, and the frock coat. All fit him perfectly now. When he heard some commotion in the street, he looked out. From what he could tell, the judge had arrived and was about to open the court session. Law headed for the courthouse.

He stood in the back, leaning against the wall, and watched through slitted eyes when McCracken led a manacled Chester Kuykendall in. The case lasted barely minutes.

"Are you ready, Sheriff, Mr. Prosecutor?" Judge Fennel Kennedy asked.

"Ah, well, no, Your Honor," the lawyer handling the prosecution, Fred Martin, said. "The main witness we had planned to call has been killed." His voice was strangled.

"You have any other witnesses? Proof? Anything that will help convict this man?"

"No, sir," Martin said, hanging his head in disgust.

"Case dismissed," Judge Kennedy intoned. "Let the prisoner go."

As a furious McCracken was unlocking the manacles, the judge said, "From what I know of this case, Mr. Kuykendall, I do hope to see you again here someday when the law has what it needs to put you away."

From the back of the courtroom, Law silently watched as a smirking Kuykendall strode out of court, followed by several gun-toting sycophants.

Minutes later, Law and McCracken sat in the sheriff's office, each with a full tumbler of whiskey in hand, despite the early hour.

When they had taken several swallows of the rotgut, McCracken asked, "So, what're you gonna do now, J.T.?" He was more than a little worried about Law—and what a man of his temper might do.

CHAPTER 20

"I AIM TO make things right," Law said darkly. Before McCracken could voice any objections, the bounty man added, "I want the names of all of Kuykendall's gunmen that you know of. And I want whatever paper you have on any of 'em. That way when I confront 'em, it'll be mostly legal."

McCracken stared at him for a few moments, wondering if he should do what Law had asked.

Seeing his friend's hesitation, and having some idea of what was going on in the sheriff's mind, Law said, "If you've heard anything about me since I took to bein' a bounty man, Jess, then you'll know I just don't go shootin' men in the back. I give 'em a chance to surrender and face justice whenever possible. Too many of 'em are damn fools, though, and make a play. That's what gets 'em sent to the boneyard."

"I've heard that."

"Then you should know I'm not about to just go out there gunnin' Kuykendall's men down. I'll try to arrest 'em and bring 'em in. If I can get a few of 'em to do that, they'd like as

not be willin' to talk—maybe even testify—against Kuykendall if it keeps 'em from gettin' their necks stretched."

McCracken liked the sound of that. It would get rid of
Chester Kuykendall the proper way. Still, he wondered if it
would really work. "You think any of his men'd be willin' to
surrender?" he asked.

Law shrugged his broad shoulders and jolted down the remaining whiskey in his glass. As he poured another, he said,
"Not at first, I reckon. Most of them cockroaches're real hard
cases, I reckon. So I expect to meet a heap of resistance at
first. But I reckon that once I send a few of 'em to the bone or-
chard, some of the others might be willin' to pull their horns
in and give up the fight."

McCracken didn't have to think it over much longer. It
didn't seem likely that he would be able to get Kuykendall
any other way. And there was every chance that Kuykendall
would go wild now that he had beaten the sheriff in court.
He put down his glass and went to the wall and pulled down
the sheaf of wanted posters that had been stuck there with a
knife. He went through them, making two piles. When he was
done, he handed one stack to Law, who set down his own glass
and, with cigar in one hand, looked through the papers.

McCracken then sat writing names on a sheet of plain paper,
pausing regularly to think, chewing on the end of the pencil
when he did. Finally he tossed the pencil down and handed the
sheet to Law. "Don't know if that list'll help you any, J.T.," the
sheriff said. "I don't expect you to know any of those names,
and without handbills on 'em, they're considered law-abidin'."

Law glanced up and nodded, then went back to looking at
the wanted posters, most of which had crudely drawn pictures
of the fugitives. Finally he put them down and looked at Mc-
Cracken. He had wondered at first why McCracken had never
gone out after any of these men, but as he had scanned the papers, it became obvious. None of these men was wanted for
anything bad. Most of the rewards were small—a hundred
dollars or less. If Law were the sheriff, he wouldn't risk his
neck or those of his deputies trying to arrest these men on
such minor warrants.

"As you may have surmised," McCracken said dryly, figuring he knew what was going through Law's mind, "we've never really had anybody identify those men in connection with any major crimes."

Law nodded, understanding. "Don't matter none, though," he said. "This is enough for me to go huntin' 'em. If they have any smarts, they'll come along peaceable, which'd be a problem. They do that, the court'll just sentence 'em to some small time in jail—I doubt if they'd even get time in the state prison. Hell, they might just have to pay a fine, and they'd be done with it." He smiled grimly. "But I don't figure none of these boys to be that smart. Besides, most of 'em think highly of themselves, so they'll be figurin' that, bein' such bad men as they are in their minds, there's bound to be warrants for 'em for more serious crimes than what's on these handbills."

"I reckon you're right, but it'd be a good thing if a couple of 'em would just come on in where I could maybe convince 'em to talk. Ah, well, we'll see what happens. You need anything from me, J.T.?"

"Reckon not."

McCracken lifted his glass. "Here's to a successful venture, pard."

The two clinked glasses and then drained the liquor in them.

Law stood, papers in one hand, cigar in the other. He folded the wanted posters and shoved them into an inside coat pocket. "Be talkin' to you, Jess," he said as he stepped out into the oppressive heat. Law walked slowly down to O'Fallon's and had Toby saddled. He rode out of Big Spring, heading southwest.

When he was still more than a mile from Kuykendall's Double Bar K ranch, Law spotted three riders coming toward him. He slowed when he was within fifty feet of them. They all stopped with barely three yards separating him from the three men.

"You lost?" the man in the middle asked.

Law recognized him as Bart Quaid. He was one of the ones with a reward on him. The other two were not among those on the wanted posters Law had. At least the ones with pictures on them. Both were young, not even as old as Blackstone had been, and looked inexperienced, though they tried to come across as hard cases. Law guessed that they were brothers.

"I got a warrant for your arrest, Quaid," Law said.

The two young men joined in the outlaw's laughter.

"You other two boys're free to go," Law said evenly. "I'd advise you to do so. I'd further advise you to find different company to keep than this riffraff you been runnin' with."

"Who you callin' riffraff, boy?" Quaid asked, a snarl curling his beefy face.

"You," Law responded flatly. "Now I'd be obliged if you was to come along peaceable."

Quaid laughed a bit more, though there was no humor in it this time. "Just who the hell are you, boy?" he demanded.

"Name's John Thomas Law."

"Never heard . . . wait a minute, you're a bounty man, ain't you? Supposed to be some real hard-ass."

"That's right, bub." He glanced from one of the young men to the other. "I really do advise you two punks to ride out. You're too young to die out here for a scrofulous piece of shit like Kuykendall, who don't give one slim goddamn hoot about you." His gaze returned to Quaid. "So what's it gonna be, bub?"

But it was one of the young men—the one to Law's left— who moved first. He jerked out his pistol, impressing his two companions with his speed. But the fast draw did little for accuracy as he fired off two quick shots.

Law drew the big Colt .45 from his belt holster and calmly put an end to the young gunman's life with one well-placed shot. The bullet ripped a chunk out of the man's head above and slightly to the left of his left eye. He fell out of the saddle. His horse, nervous, shifted uneasily, but stood its ground.

Quaid and his companion unlimbered their pistols as well, but their horses were shuffling nervously. The young man's animal reared, neighing wildly. Both men fired, but with no effect, as they fought to control their unruly mounts.

Law was glad he had Toby beneath him. The horse was time-tested and steady, and completely trusted the man on its back. Law pulled the reins and moved Toby to the side a little, where Law had a more open shot at both adversaries.

A shot from Quaid tore a hole in one of the tails of Law's new frock coat. Law returned fire but missed when Quaid's horse skittered backward a few steps. Law fired again. Quaid was, he figured, the more dangerous of the two men, what with his experience and age, so he wanted to get him first. But the target was moving too much, and the bullet missed its mark.

Law was ready to take another shot at Quaid, but a bullet fired by the young man ripped through Law's hat, sending it flying, and Law swiftly turned his attention to him. He fired twice, then a third time.

The young man flopped backward across the saddle's cantle, the reins falling from his lifeless fingers. The horse tried to dart off but stepped in a hole after a few feet and tumbled forward, screaming when its leg snapped. The rider's body was flung forward, like a corn-husk doll, where it bounced and rolled in the dirt.

Law didn't see it. As soon as the horse bolted, Law's attention immediately swung back to Quaid, who managed to get off another shot in the bounty man's general direction. But his horse was more skittish than ever, and Quaid was having trouble trying to regain control of the animal.

Law would not give the hardened outlaw another chance. He jammed the empty Peacemaker back into the holster and grabbed the smaller version from the shoulder rig. He brought the revolver up and fired three times.

Quaid flinched involuntarily as each bullet hit him. He dropped his weapon but managed to keep ahold of the reins. He sat in the saddle, weaving, dead, though his mind would not accept it. Then he fell to the side, off the horse, landing with a thud.

Law moved over quickly and grabbed the horse's reins. He dismounted, knowing Toby would stay where he was. He tied the reins to Quaid's horse around one of the animal's forelegs. Then he walked to the horse of the first gunman he had shot. It took some minutes of coaxing, but he got that horse calmed down, too, and hobbled it the same way as the other.

He walked over and shot the horse that had broken its leg, then reloaded both pistols. He dragged the young man's body from the dead horse to where the other horses were. He placed it and his brother's body's on the brother's horse and tied them down.

Rummaging in his saddlebags, he pulled out a piece of blank paper and a pencil. Using his saddle as a makeshift desk, he wrote: "Justice is mine, J.T. Law." He found a jack-knife in one of Quaid's pockets, opened it, and used it to stick the note to the body of one of the young men. Then he slapped the horse's rump, sending it running in the direction of Kuy-kendall's ranch.

He finally tossed Quaid's corpse across his horse and lashed it down. He mounted Toby and headed back to Big Spring, riding right up Main Street and stopping in front of McCracken's office. Inside, he slapped Quaid's wanted poster on his friend's desk. "The seventy-five dollars on Quaid's head wasn't hardly worth my time," Law said dryly. "But the battle is drawn." He explained what had happened.

McCracken grinned. "I ain't usually a cruel man, J.T.," he said, "but damn if I don't like you sendin' Kuykendall that note like you done. It's too bad those young men had to die, but they chose their fate."

"Bad choice," Law allowed.

McCracken nodded. "What now, J.T.?"

"I aim to get me a decent meal and a bottle of hooch. Might even get me a woman. Then rest up from my labors. Come mornin', I'll pay the Double Bar K a visit."

JESSAMINE, THE CYPRIAN, spotted Law as soon as he entered the Wellspring Saloon and walked to a table where he could sit with his back to the wall. She smiled brightly at him, then said a few words to the man she was standing at the bar with. His face darkened, but she either didn't notice or didn't care, leaving him fuming there as she grabbed a bottle from the bar and headed for Law.

"Howdy, sweetheart," she said with a dazzling grin as she set the bottle on the table and perched on his lap. "Miss me?"

Law cracked a smile. "It's why I'm back," he said huskily. Over her shoulder, he could see the man she had been with approaching his table, accompanied by another. "But for now, you best take your own seat."

"But . . . why . . . ?" She looked over and saw the two well-heeled men heading their way. She scooted off Law's lap and onto the chair next to him.

With his left hand, Law surreptitiously undid the buttons of his frock coat. With his right, he swept the side of the garment away from the pistol at his hip. With his right hand resting on his thigh and his left on the table, he waited.

"Me and that there woman got business, mister," the one man said, words a bit slurred.

"That ain't true, Tim," Jessamine protested sweetly.

"Shut your flappin' hole, bitch," Tim said. "I wasn't talkin' to you. I was talkin' to this asshole here." He pointed at Law,

"Damn," Law said in mock amazement, "you really know how to sweet-talk women, don't you, bub?"

"Just keep your nose out of my business, punk." He finally looked at Jessamine. "Let's go, bitch."

The fake grin dropped from Law's face. "You're treadin' on shaky ground here, Fitzgibbons," he said, putting the face to a name on one of the wanted posters in his pocket.

"You're beginnin' to annoy hell out of . . . How the hell do you know who I am?"

"There's a reward out for you, Fitzgibbons," Law said. "A measly fifty bucks, but it'd be enough to pay for an evenin' or two with this fine lady here. Now, I ain't really disposed to disrupt my night with arrestin' you and takin' you over to the jail right now, so I suggest you do it yourself and save me the effort. And take your idiot friend with you, too." Law recognized the other man as Asa Gibney, who also was worth only fifty dollars.

Fitzgibbons let go a laugh that sounded like a donkey. "That's rich," he said when the braying had ended. "You got a sense of humor, mister. That's a rare thing these days. But it'll only take you so far when you're interferin' with my business." Without taking his eyes off Law, he said over his shoulder, "I'm tired of this. Grab the whore, Asa, and let's go have us a good time."

Gibney headed around the table, reaching out for Jessamine, while Fitzgibbons glared at Law, a smirk on his face, as if daring Law to do something.

CHAPTER 21

LAW SNATCHED OUT the .45 from the shoulder holster, thumbed back the hammer, and had it pointed at the middle of Fitzgibbons's pocked face in one smooth, swift motion. He had had enough of Kuykendall's men for one day. He was hot, a bit tired—and still angry as a wounded bear over his failure to keep Hank Blackstone safe. Meaning he was not of any kind of humor to play patty-cake with the two fools.

Fitzgibbons's eyes widened in surprise, then lowered in anger. Gibney stopped moving and stood very still.

"Perhaps you've gone a bit deaf, Mr. Fitzgibbons," Law said in an icy voice. "The woman don't want to go with you and your halfwit *amigo* there. Now you got a choice to make here—and be assured that it's a life-and-death decision, pard. Get the hell away from me, and stay away from me—and Jessamine—or . . ." He wiggled the muzzle of the Colt a fraction of an inch. "So what's it gonna be, bub?"

Fitzgibbons was sweating, though it wasn't from the heat. "Just take it easy there, mister," he said, raising his hands in a form of surrender, trying to buy some time.

"Make up your mind, lard ass," Law snapped, weapon un-wavering, held steady by his resting elbow on the table. "I've already sent several of your cronies to the boneyard today. I ain't above addin' two more to the list."

Asa Gibney ever so slowly began moving his hand toward his holstered wood-handled Remington. He was barely breath-ing, not wanting to attract Law's notice, hoping his friend could keep the bounty man occupied a little bit longer. Just until he could draw the revolver. Streams of sweat rolled down from under his hat and dripped off his nose, but he forced himself to keep moving like molasses. He was almost there. He just needed a few more moments. His hand brushed the butt of the pistol and began curling around it.

Though he had not taken his eyes off Fitzgibbons, he was well aware of what Gibney was doing. And as soon as Gib-ney's hand starting closing on the pistol grip, Law fired.

The bullet from Law's Peacemaker smashed into the tiny space between Fitzgibbons's nose and his left eye. The eyeball popped out as Fitzgibbons staggered back a few steps, and the lead bullet made a bloody mess coming out the back of the man's head and smashed a bottle sitting on the bar. Fitzgib-bons fell, dead without ever realizing what was happening.

Law swiveled toward Gibney, who was drawing his re-volver, though it was only halfway out of the holster.

Law did not hesitate. He fired once, shattering Gibney's head like a melon bashed with a sledgehammer. He had no re-grets about it. He had given these men several chances to walk away from trouble, but they had been too foolish to take them.

Law started to slide the Colt back into the shoulder holster when he caught some movement out of the corner of his right eye. Not knowing what it was, but not wanting to take any chances, he yanked the gun out with his right hand, and shoved Jessamine hard with his left.

She fell off the chair with a yelp, Law following her. Half lying on top of her, he turned and kicked the table over on its side, just as he heard a gunshot.

A bullet tore through the tabletop, barely missing him. He scrabbled around onto his knees and then popped up over the edge of the table for just a second to try to spot where the gunfire was coming from. As he ducked back behind the table, two more bullets ripped through it, one digging up wood from the floor, the other breezing by his head.

But Law had seen his target—a man standing thirty feet away, a Smith & Wesson in his hand. Law plopped onto his butt and lashed out with both boots, kicking a chair over as a distraction. Then he immediately shoved himself to his feet, firing off two shots as he came to a stop in a crouch.

The enemy's arm jerked to the side, and his gun went flying as one bullet smashed its way through the forearm. The other bullet hit him in the chest, knocking him back a couple of steps.

Law moved forward slowly, gun partly lowered. His eyes swept the room for other potential foes, but no one seemed as if he was going to make a move. At ten feet from the gun-man, Law raised his Colt and fired once more, putting a bullet in the man's brain.

The man crumpled.

Hearing the door swing open, Law spun and crouched, shifting the almost empty small Colt to his left hand, and drawing the weapon's big brother in his right, cocking it.

Town Marshal Fred Langenfeld came to a sudden stop when he saw Law. His eyes grew wide as a jolt of fear burst through him.

Blowing out his breath, Law rose to his full height. He looked around, once more making sure no one was about to try to kill him. Then he shoved his pistols into their holsters and walked over to the table where he had been sitting. He offered Jessamine his hand. She allowed him to help her up. She seemed shaken, but not nearly as rattled as the marshal appeared to be.

"Still of a mind to have a good time?" he asked.

She smiled. "I am," she said. She took Law's proffered arm.

They walked over and stopped in front of Langenfeld. The marshal stood, almost shaking, though he had put his pistol away. "You want to tell me what went on here, Law?" he demanded, trying to sound as if he had control of the situation.

"Varmint shootin'," Law said dryly. "All three of 'em have warrants out on 'em. They're all Kuykendall's men, too," he added, voice growing harsh. "Since you're in cahoots with that villainous bastard, next time you talk with him, you tell him that he *will* face justice." He started to walk away.

Langenfeld grabbed him by the coat sleeve. "Now, you just wait one goddamn minute there, boy," the marshal said, bristling. When he saw the deadly look in Law's piercing blue-green eyes, he let go of the garment. But he was still angry when he demanded, "What makes you think I'm in cahoots with Kuykendall?"

"Jess says you won't do anything about him or his boys. And when I brought Billy Crawford into your office, you acted like I was the one in the wrong. What's a man to think?"

"Kuykendall ain't done nothin' wrong in Big Spring," Langenfeld said defensively. "And Billy, well, he's just a minor troublemaker, not—"

"That's a heapin' pile of horse apples, Marshal, and you damn well know it. You maybe can lie to the people of Big Spring, and you can maybe lie to yourself, but I ain't believin' a word of it."

"You don't know the whole of it."

"Maybe not. I just know you ain't done your job. If you had, some damned good people would still be alive. Now, make sure Jess McCracken learns of this so I can get my money."

"Blood money," Langenfeld said with distaste.

"Well-earned, bub," Law snapped. "You did your job, I wouldn't have had to." Law turned and, with Jessamine on his arm, headed out into the night.

"SOUNDS LIKE YOU had a right lively night, J.T.," Mc-Cracken said the next morning.

Law was eating breakfast in the Llano House's restaurant, and the sheriff had joined him moments ago.

"Yep." He grinned. "That Jessamine is—"

McCracken laughed. "I didn't mean that," he allowed. "Though I bet that's a far more interestin' story. So what happened over at the Wellspring?"

Law explained it.

"Reckon it couldn't be helped," McCracken said, unconcerned that three more of Kuykendall's men had been removed.

He poured himself a cup of coffee and sipped some. "I do expect Kuykendall will be frothin' at the mouth when Fred Langenfeld tells him."

"I expect so. But I ain't so sure Langenfeld'd be the one to tell him."

"You don't think the marshal's on Kuykendall's payroll?" McCracken asked as he grabbed a biscuit.

"Doesn't Lucy Mae feed you?" Law inquired.

"A growin' boy's got to eat." McCracken grinned as he slathered butter on the biscuit.

"Growin' fat is more like it." Law poured himself more coffee.

"So what's this about you not thinkin' Langenfeld is one of Kuykendall's boys?"

"Just a hunch, Jess," Law said around a mouthful of beefsteak and eggs. "He got his back up when I hinted at that last night."

"Which would be expected."

"Granted. But somethin' about him just made me think different. You know what it is? I think he's just a lily-livered cockroach who's afraid of his own shadow. Man like that is gonna do anythin' to keep from puttin' his life in danger."

McCracken thought about that as he chewed on the biscuit, then shrugged. "You might be right." He ate a moment, then asked, "You aimin' to pay a visit out there to the Double Bar K today?"

"Yep," Law said with a tight nod. "If Kuykendall don't know yet that he's up against this tough old wolf, he's gonna know it soon."

"You just watch yourself out there. You're good, J.T., maybe even the best. But you're still mighty outgunned."

"I'll be careful. I got no hankerin' to die of lead poisonin'."

JUST AS HE was about to head for Kuykendall's ranch, Law decided he had something else to do first, a promise to keep. He trotted out of town on the road heading east. An hour and a half later, he rode into Mustang and stopped in front of the marshal's office. No one was inside, so he went to the hardware emporium next door.

"You Carl Bockman?" he asked of the man who greeted him.

"Yah." Fright showed on his face as he took in Law's size, armament, and hard look. "Who vants to know?"

"Name's J.T. Law. I'm a friend of Hank Blackstone's." Pain and anger crossed his face.

"He is goink to be buried today," Bockman said sadly.

"I know. But that ain't why I'm here. It's my fault he's dead, but I made him a promise that I intend to keep. Which is why I'm here."

"How can I help?" Bockman asked. Whatever fear he had had was gone. He instinctively felt as if he could trust this man.

"Where's Marshal Endicott?"

"Ach, dot useless fellow. He's probably still feedink his fat face at Celia's restaurant down the street. Vhy do you vant the marshal?"

Law ignored the question. He touched the brim of his hat and said, "Obliged." He turned and left, walking up the street, eyes scanning everyone, frightening most of them.

Moments later he spotted the marshal, who saw him about the same time and hesitated. He didn't know Law, but he was sure he meant trouble.

"You got a lot to account for, Marshal," Law said flatly.

"What the hell're you talkin' about?" Endicott demanded, uncertainty showing on his face.

"Because of your evil doin's, several good people and a couple of innocent children are dead. And it's time you paid for those misdeeds."

"What the hell're you talkin' about?" Endicott repeated. He was almost shaking now.

"If you got any sense in that fat head of yours, bub," Law said harshly, "you'll take off that badge and drop your gun belt and come with me."

"If I don't?" Endicott tried bravado with a notable lack of success.

"Then you'll die here in the street like the dog you are."

"I don't know what the hell you're talkin' about," Endicott tried again. "I—"

"Either surrender or pull your piece, you pile of filth."

Endicott could hear his death in that voice, and he was shaken to his roots. "But, I—"

Law drew a pistol and shot Endicott in the left leg, just above the knee.

Endicott screamed as his leg buckled and he sank to his knees. "Please, mister . . ."

Law was disgusted. This man had not even the slightest shred of dignity. "Do you submit?" he asked.

"Who the hell are you?" Endicott asked, shaking with fear now. He looked around, hoping someone in the large crowd that had gathered would help him. He saw no sympathy in any-one's eyes.

"You know who I am and why I'm here, you scurrilous wretch. Now surrender so I can take you to Big Spring to stand trial."

"You're *loco,* mister. Whoever you are."

Law was about to reply when he saw a change in the mar-shal's eyes, going from terror to almost smugness. Law sud-denly whirled, dropping into a fighting crouch as he brought his pistol up. He fired twice as he saw the deputy marshal coming up on him fast, gun in hand.

The deputy died with two bullets in the head, without even knowing he had been hit.

Law spun back to face Endicott, who had yanked out his pistol. He was trying to aim it with shaky hands when Law put two lead slugs into his chest.

Law jammed the pistol back into the holster, walked over, and pulled himself into the saddle on Toby. He backed the horse into the center of the street, where the animal shuffled, shaking his great mane.

"Marshal Endicott and his deputy were workin' for Chester Kuykendall," Law roared. "Because of them, Hank Black-stone and his whole family—includin' two innocent little ones—are dead. You're now free of these two men's taint. And lest any of you others are thinkin' to side with Kuykendall, let me assure you, his days are numbered."

Law wheeled the horse and galloped out of Mustang. He stopped in Big Spring just long enough to tell McCracken,

"Mustang needs a new marshal," before riding out toward the Kuykendall spread. As he moved onto the outer fringes of the Double Bar K, he encountered two of Kuykendall's men.

"You must be the famous bounty man, John Thomas Law," the one, whom Law identified as Nate Carter, said.

"I am. And if you know that, you know I'm gonna ask you to give yourselves up peaceable and let me take you in to face justice."

"Afraid we can't do that, boy."

As Carter raised the scattergun that had been lying across the front of his saddle, Law jabbed his heels into Toby's sides. The horse jumped forward, plowing between the two gunmen's horses, startling them. Law galloped on a few yards, then swung around. He looped the reins loosely around the saddle horn. Then, taking one of his pistols in each hand, he charged forward, like in the old days. It was exhilarating as he rode down on these men who were trying to control their horses and fire—Carter the shotgun, the other man a pistol.

Carter stood his ground, finally managing to get the scattergun up to his shoulder, but it was too late. Two bullets from one of Law's .45s punctured his chest and throat, and he died right off.

The other man had turned when he saw Law coming from behind him and raced off the way he had been facing, instead of turning to meet Law. The bounty man rode hard behind him, the reliable Toby closing the distance fast. Not wanting to shoot the man in the back, Law raced past him, then jerked Toby to a sharp halt. He spun in the saddle and fired, putting two bullets in the man's chest.

The man fell. Law dismounted. With pistol still in hand and ready, he approached the downed gunman, whom, he found, was still alive. Law knelt next to him, relieving the man of his pistol, which he tossed out into the grass. "There anything you'd like to say before you meet your maker?" he asked. He knew the man would not last more than a few minutes.

"Only that you'll get yours, you bastard," the man gasped. "Mr. Kuykendall has men all over the place out here lookin' for you."

Law gazed off into the distance. "Then he's gonna have a

hell of a lot more dead men on his hands," he said. But the gunman didn't hear him.

Law reloaded his pistols, then put the bodies of the men he had just killed on their horses, and strung them together, then rode on. While he had been vigilant before, he was even more so now.

By dark, Law had covered a fair piece of ground on the lookout for more of Kuykendall's men. He had come across none, though, and was ready to return to Big Spring. But as he crested a small hump of grassy earth, he thought he spotted the flicker of a small fire in the distance. He wasn't sure, but he was determined to find out. He rode slowly toward it under the pale, silvery moonlight, stopping when he was about fifty yards away, knowing now that it was a fire.

He hobbled the horses and took off his coat, tying it onto the saddle with his bedroll. Leaving Toby behind, he ran in a crouch until he was within fifty feet of the fire, which was, obviously, a small camp. He slowed and crept forward until he could hear voices. He stopped and listened for a few minutes, grinning savagely in the darkness as he caught snatches of conversation:

"I wonder if Nate or Butch or any of the others got that bastard Law."

"If they did, I wish they'd come tell us so we could go back to the bunkhouse. Feedin' there'd be a powerful lot better than eatin' this slop."

That was greeted with a little laughter. There was some talk that Law could not distinguish, then, "I hear this feller we're lookin' for, this J.T. Law, is one tough *hombre*."

"I hear he's a back-shootin' son of a bitch."

Law stiffened at the last comment. Relegating his anger to a spot deep inside him where it would simmer until needed without causing him to make foolish mistakes, he edged forward. In the low light of the fire, he could see eight horses tied to a large, spreading mesquite.

"Back-shootin' son of a bitch, am I?" he breathed. He rose up to his full six foot two. "We'll just see about that." He eased out both pistols and cocked them.

CHAPTER 22

✦

LAW MOVED LIKE a wraith just outside the ring of firelight. The first time the eight men sitting around the fire knew he was there was when he said softly but with force, "Evenin', boys. My name is John Thomas Law. I'm here to bring you to justice. You're all advised to surrender your guns and submit to arrest."

It took several moments before that sank in, and then the eight men moved. Some went for their guns where they were, others dove for the darkness before drawing their weapons.

At the first sign of movement, Law opened fire, alternating shots from each Peacemaker, until both were down to one cartridge each. He was pretty certain he had hit at least five of the men in the first few seconds, though he didn't know whether he had killed them or just wounded them.

He spun and silently moved several paces to his left, where he stopped and squatted. He reloaded the two Colts, his practiced fingers having no difficulty in the dark; he had become well versed in doing so when he was a guerrilla rider for the Southern cause. As he worked he heard two horses galloping off.

His eyes had adjusted, and he was able to see a little in the dim light of the moon. He did not look directly at the fire, but he saw no movement in the general vicinity of it.

Suddenly someone plowed into him from behind, slamming him forward onto his face in the dirt and rough, dry grass. He managed to keep his grip on both pistols, even as he lashed out with an elbow. There was a satisfying thwack as it connected with flesh and bone, eliciting a grunt.

Law rolled over onto his back and half sitting up, he reached out the smaller Colt and fired once.

A dark figure howled and fell back.

Law jumped up and moved forward, fast. He knelt next to the black shape on the ground and stuck the muzzle of the cocked Peacemaker under the man's chin. "Quit or die, boy," he growled, not even sure that the man was still alive.

"It don't matter none," the man said in a frightened whisper. "I'm dyin' anyway."

"Where're you hit?"

"Neck. It hurts like all hellfire."

After slipping the big Colt away, Law began running his right hand over the man's neck. As he did so, he asked him, "What's your name, boy?"

"Sven Halverson." He flinched when Law's hand hit a tender spot.

"Well, Mr. Halverson," Law allowed as he probed the tender spot on the man's neck, "I don't think you're gonna die today. Unless you come at me again."

"I ain't gonna die?" Halverson asked, his blue eyes shining where they caught the moonlight.

"Nope."

"But my neck."

"Bullet just grazed you. I know it hurts like hell, but it ain't fatal. Now sit up and put your hands behind your back." When Halverson did, Law tied his hands there, using Halverson's own bandanna. While he worked, Law asked, "Why didn't you just shoot me, boy? Would've made a lot more sense than tryin' to whup me, even if you are near as big as I am."

"Lost my gun in the dark," Halverson responded with regret in his voice.

"Your bad luck, bub. Stand up." When both were on their feet, Law said, "Call out to your friends. See if any of 'em responds. You say anything to warn 'em, and you'll die right here."

Halverson called out a string of names. The only response was one pain-racked groan from near the fire. Law wasn't sure someone wasn't sitting out there in the darkness, keeping quiet, just waiting for a shot at him, but he didn't think so. He would have to go under the assumption that it wasn't true.

"All right, let's go to the fire." As they moved, Law placed his left hand on Halverson's shoulder, keeping him in front of him. Law also had his pistol out, and cocked, though he carried it at arm's length straight down. "Sit next to the fire, boy, where I can keep an eye on you." Law ordered.

The bounty man grabbed a few mesquite sticks and tossed them on the flames, building up the fire so he could see better. Then he checked the area. He found five men, four of them dead, one of them clinging to life, but he would not make it through the night; maybe not even the next hour. If two had ridden off, as Law had heard, the five here and Halverson accounted for them all.

He began to relax a little, though not too much. There was still a lot to be done, and he had to hurry. He figured the two who had gotten away were riding like hell for Kuykendall's ranch and would be just as quick as they could with reinforcements.

Ignoring the saddles, Law simply began tossing bodies on horses and tying them down.

As Law worked, Halverson said, "What're you gonna do with me, mister?"

"Take you into Big Spring and turn you over to Sheriff Mc-Cracken. I don't know if there's any warrants out for you, but I expect we can find somethin' to charge you with. Assaultin' me, if nothin' else. Of course, if you got any sense a'tall, boy, you'll talk with Sheriff McCracken and tell him what you know of that cockroach Kuykendall and the scurrilous activities he's been up to."

"But I don't know—"

"Don't lie to me, boy. Just cogitate on it some while you're sittin' there."

Law helped Halverson onto his horse, bareback, then strung all the horses together. Taking some extra rope, which he looped over his shoulder, Law walked the horses to where Toby and the other two horses were. He roped the new animals to the old, then mounted Toby and headed for Big Spring, moving as fast as he dared.

As dawn began to make its dim appearance, Law realized that he was still almost a mile from the town. He had hoped to be there by now. He rubbed a hand over his face, feeling the tiredness of a long day followed by a night with no sleep.

He pushed on, but he soon saw four horseman ahead. He slowed a little, wondering if they were some kind of welcoming committee from the town. Then he stopped and got out the telescope. They were still a few hundred yards away, but they had spotted him and were coming fast toward him. As happened often out here, they disappeared for some moments in a dip, then reappeared again. He sat there for a few minutes, watching, then realized they were no townsfolk.

Law stood in the stirrups and looked around, trying to find some place where he could make a stand. But there was nothing. He collapsed the telescope and shoved it into a saddlebag,

"Hey, Mr. Law," Halverson called. "What's goin' on? Why're we stopped?"

Law glanced back at him. "Seems like some of your pukin' friends are headin' this way to pay their respects to me." His glare cut off any further conversation.

Law turned back to the front. He patted his horse on the neck. "I know you're tired, Toby, but we got us some serious business facin' us here."

The horse nickered softly and shook his great head.

Law dismounted and hurriedly hobbled a couple of the horses. With them all being tied together, they would not be able to go anywhere. Then he jumped into the saddle and kicked Toby into a run. As he neared the rushing men, he wrapped the reins around the saddle horn and drew both revolvers.

He charged on, ignoring the gunfire directed at him since he was still out of range of pistols. He held his fire until he was within seventy-five feet of the onrushing group, which had spread out a little. Then he opened up, firing with calm deadliness. It was as if he were back with Bill Quantrill or Bill Anderson, taking on some Yankee cavalry.

He hit one man, who fell off his horse and lay still after bouncing a few times. Then he hit a second, but that man did not fall. He did stop, though, and just sat on his horse, wrists crossed on the saddle horn, watching.

A slug tore through one shirtsleeve, and another cracked through the outside of a stirrup. His hat flew off, and Law was not sure if the wind or a bullet was responsible.

Law split the two remaining riders and several yards beyond got Toby to stop. He swung around, swiftly reloading his pistols. By the time he had done so, the two gunmen had also turned and were charging at him again. He got Toby going again, racing forward. And he fired three times from each pistol, knocking both from their horses, which continued running.

Law shoved one pistol away and took the reins, bringing Toby to a halt again. He spun, seeing the wounded man racing off in the general direction of Kuykendall's ranch. Law reloaded his weapons. Gathering up his caravans of horses, he rode to the first two bodies, tossed them up on horses with other corpses, and then got the third one and did the same.

Half an hour later, Law rode into Big Spring, right up Main Street. It was quite a spectacle, and people stopped whatever they were doing to watch this strange procession with horror or interest, as if it were a circus parade.

McCracken had heard the commotion out in the street, and stepped out of his office, with his deputy beside him. The sheriff's jaw dropped as Law stopped in front of him. "Je-sus!" McCracken said.

"I do believe Chester Kuykendall's stable of gunmen has been considerably depleted," Law said.

"I reckon that's true," McCracken commented, still amazed. He had seen John Thomas Law do some pretty incredible things in battle during the war, but he never expected anything like this. "Charlie," he said to his deputy, "take these bodies over to the Trigueras brothers. Tell Pedro that they're to get the cheapest treatment and to send the bill to Kuykendall."

"Yes, sir." That was about the only thing that awed Charlie

Collins was able to say at the moment. He walked, stunned, to take the rope to the string of horses from Law.

"Best cut Mr. Halverson loose first, Charlie," Law suggested.

The deputy nodded absently and cut Halverson's horse loose. Then he led the others away, walking up the street. He was regaining some sense of normality and began shouting at the nosy people to get out of the way.

McCracken went inside. Nudging Halverson ahead of him, Law followed. Law cut the bandanna off of the young man's hands and told him to sit. "Jess," Law said, "this here is Sven Halverson. I ain't certain, you understand, but he might be willin' to shed some light on Kuykendall's activities. I suggested to him that doin' so would be a good thing, and he's had some time to think it over."

"Well?" McCracken questioned, looking at Halverson.

The big, broad-shouldered young man had, indeed, given it considerable thought. He wanted so very much to refuse to do so, to prove that he was loyal to the man who had allowed him to become a hard case, a man people feared. But after Law's performance at his camp last night and during the attack a little while ago, that resolve had dissipated. John Thomas Law had killed about a dozen of Kuykendall's best gunmen in the past twenty-four hours. And if talk around the bunkhouse had any truth to it, he had killed a number of others.

Halverson nodded.

"Good," McCracken said. "First, though, here's the money for those others you brought to heel, J.T." He held out some greenbacks and set a piece of paper on the end of the desk. "Need you to sign that, too, acknowledgin' that you got your money."

Law did so.

"And I'll start the paperwork on these others directly, soon's we're sure who they are."

Law nodded.

"You aim to stay while I question this fella?" McCracken pointed at Halverson.

"Reckon not. I got a heap of things to do, and I'm long overdue on some shut-eye." Law left the office, rode to the livery, and made sure O'Fallon knew that Toby was to get an extra ration of oats and the best treatment possible. He also left instructions to have the stirrup replaced.

Then he walked to Wentworth's, aware that people were continuing to talk about him in hushed tones wherever he went. At Wentworth's, he bought another new frock coat and a hat. He visited the seamstress so she could tailor his coat. He next went to the Llano House's restaurant, where he filled up on two steaks, two helpings of potatoes, some beans, and half a dozen biscuits, washed down with a pint of beer and then three cups of strong, black coffee.

Full, he went to the barbershop for a long, hot bath and a shave and had his hair trimmed. At long last, he entered his room at the Llano House, closing the door on the world behind him. He wanted nothing more than to sleep, but his work was not yet finished. He set about taking care of his two Colts, carefully breaking them down, cleaning them, oiling them, and then reloading them. He hung the shoulder holster on the bedpost, took off his gun belt and put it on a chair, after taking the weapon and sticking it under his pillow. He pulled off his boots and took off his vest. With a sigh, he stretched out on the soft bed.

He did not know how long he had been asleep when a knock at the door woke him. It was still light, so he figured it was early afternoon. He shook his head to clear the cobwebs as the knock came again, a timid rapping.

Law rose, grabbing the big Peacemaker from under the pillow. Holding the cocked revolver behind his back, he walked silently in stocking feet to the door. The knock came again.

Standing just to the left of the door, he reached out and gently turned the knob. Then, he suddenly jerked the door open, and spun around it, bringing the gun up and out at arm's length.

CHAPTER 23

THE FRIGHT THAT leaped onto the visitor's face did nothing to disguise the fact that she was the most beautiful woman Law had ever seen. Large, glittering, coal-black eyes; long, wavy raven hair; dark, creamy skin; heart-shaped face; full lips.

Law's eyes swept downward just a bit over the brown, bare shoulders on which the day's heat had left a sheen of perspiration that trailed down to the deep, chocolate cleavage.

The woman batted her eyes a couple of times and seemed to regain her composure faster than he did. "You are Mr. Law?" she asked, her voice dripping honey and with a light, enticing accent. "Mr. John Thomas Law?" She was doing a hell of a job ignoring the Peacemaker still pointed at her head.

"Yep." Law tried to pull himself together. "And you are?"

"Lorita Kuykendall. I must talk with you."

For the second time in less than a minute, Law was shocked. He lifted the muzzle of his pistol to the roof and moved a step to the side, giving her room. "Come in, Mrs. Kuykendall."

"Please call me Lorita," she said as she stepped lightly inside with a swish of skirts.

Law swiftly but carefully poked his head outside the door and looked both ways. He saw no one. He backed into the room, shut the door, and turned. He eased the hammer of the Colt down. He grabbed the chair and moved it a little, turning it to face the bed. With his left hand he indicated that Lorita should sit. She did.

He hesitated in putting the pistol down. In was not every day that a woman of Lorita Kuykendall's extraordinary beauty came knocking at his door asking to talk to him, and considering who her husband was, he did not put a lot of trust in her. Giving her another lingering look, he realized that the only place she could be hiding a gun would be strapped to her leg, and if she was, she would have to dig under the dress and half a dozen petticoats to get at it. He tossed the .45 on the bed.

"I'm sorry I don't have anything to offer you to drink, Mrs. . . . ah, Lorita," he said quietly.

Her eyes flickered to the whiskey bottle on the night table and then back to him.

His brows rose, but he shrugged and poured her two fingers of whiskey into one of the two glasses and handed it to her. Then he poured himself a slightly more generous serving in the other glass. Each took a sip as Law plunked his big form down on the bed. "Now, Miz Lorita, you said you wanted to talk to me?"

"I believe that you are the man carrying out a bloody vendetta against my husband."

"It ain't a vendetta really," Law offered after a moment of staring at her with raised eyebrows. He didn't much like being called a cold-blooded killer in so many words, even by a woman of Lorita's beauty. "Just doin' my job and helpin' some friends." He had come here in the first place to help Jess McCracken, and he thought the late Hank Blackstone could be considered a friend after what had happened. "I would agree it's a bloody business, though, ma'am. But it's your no-'count husband who's responsible for that."

"You don't like my husband very much, do you, Mr. Law?" She took a sip of whiskey, her dark, enthralling eyes peering over the rim of the glass.

"At the risk of offendin' you, ma'am, I think your husband

is a murderous scoundrel, the spawn of the devil, and needs to be crushed like an insect. He is responsible for the deaths of a number of very fine people and even some innocent children. Barely more than babies." His anger was bubbling to the surface, and he clapped his mouth shut lest it burst out.

Lorita took another sip of whiskey, then smiled brightly. "I was hoping you'd say something of that nature."

This woman was full of surprises, Law thought. "And why is that?" he asked.

"Because, Mr. Law, it tells me that I've made the right decision in coming here."

"Oh?" Law was befuddled, only partly because of Lorita's cryptic comments.

"I agree with your assessment of my husband, Mr. Law," Lorita said. "He's an evil man. It was bad when he treated me as poorly as he did for so many years, but when I learned of what he was doing . . . Well, I had to do something." She finished off the whiskey and put the glass down, then patted her lips demurely with a small, lace-edged handkerchief. "There was a problem, though." She smiled almost shyly. "I didn't know what to do or how to do it." Once more she favored Law with a dazzling smile. "Then you came along."

"And what does my coming along have to do with it?" Law asked, suspicious again.

"I need your help, Mr. Law. I want to leave my husband, but I'm afraid to as long as he's free to do his will."

"I don't kill people just on someone's whim, Lorita," Law said quietly.

She looked disappointed but said, "I understand." Her voice, her face, her figure were almost overwhelming. "In that case," she added after some thought, "it would serve me almost as well if he was to be arrested, convicted, and then hanged—or even sent to prison for the rest of his days."

"That's a heap easier said than done, ma'am."

"It shouldn't be so hard if I help you." She paused, running the tip of her tongue over her lips, fully aware of what it was doing to Law. It had the same effect on most men.

"How can you help?"

"I have access to some papers—letters mostly—that

should be enough evidence to get Chester convicted on at least a couple of bank robberies and maybe a killing or two."

"Why don't you just take them to Sheriff McCracken?" Law asked. "He'd go right out and arrest your husband."

"I might be willing to do that," Lorita said thoughtfully. "But if I did, Chester would know that I was the one responsible for him being arrested, and he'd try to have me killed as sure as anything. You know how vicious he is. But I'd still be willin' to do that—if I had some protection. Someone to watch over me until Chester was hanged or sent off to prison." She graced him with a gaze that was near to tears.

Law was intrigued. If what she said about the information was true, it would be a fine way to rid Howard County of Chester Kuykendall in a legal way. That he would have to spend time in the presence of this extraordinarily beautiful woman was a bonus. On the other hand, he thought, feelings of self-recrimination sweeping over him, he had done a mighty poor job of keeping his last charge alive. Could he do any better with Lorita Kuykendall?

Seeing his hesitation, Lorita leaned forward and touched the back of his left hand with her small, slim fingers. Heated promise burned in her eyes as she added in a husky voice, "I'd do anything for your help, Mr. Law." The tongue darted out across those full lips again. "Anything."

Law pushed down the self-doubts that had crept up with his thoughts of failing to protect Hank Blackstone, and he nodded. "All right, Miz Lorita," he said. "When can you bring the papers?"

She sat back in the chair and smiled again, the effect just as dazzling this time as it had been the first time. "I could get things together by tomorrow, I'd say." Gloom suddenly descended on her. "But I'm not sure how to get them to you. If I was to come to town again, Chester would make sure some of his men escorted me on the ride. He always does." Her voice trailed off.

"Where are they now?" Law asked, suspicions aroused again.

"Over at the Longhorn Saloon. I told them I was going to

visit a friend." She smiled slyly. "I told them she had a room here."

Law nodded, accepting it. He tried to think of some way to get around the problem.

"I suppose I . . ." She noticed the expectant look that appeared in his eyes. "Well, maybe I could slip away. I often ride around the ranch, though I don't venture far from the house. I suppose I could tell Chester I'm going to do that, and slip off without anyone being the wiser. But . . ." Her eyes clouded with doubt and worry. "But I suppose he'd realize after a while that I was gone longer than usual, and he'd send men out to find me. I don't know if I could reach Big Spring before I was found out."

Law gave that some consideration, then said, "I reckon I could meet you somewhere between the ranch and here. I could escort you the rest of the way into Big Spring." He figured that he could handle the one or two men Kuykendall might send after Lorita, if they even caught up with them. The chances of that were slim anyway.

"You'd do that?" Lorita asked, brightening, her voice and body expressing eagerness.

Law nodded.

"Oh, that would be wonderful." She rubbed her hands together in a girlish gesture that touched Law. She settled down, brow furrowed a little in thought.

"What?" Law asked, concerned.

"Oh," she said with another smile, "I'm just trying to think of a spot we can meet." She paused, then nodded. "I know. There's a big old mesquite tree on a small rise about four miles from town. It's, oh, I don't know, I guess a quarter mile south of the road to the ranch."

Law nodded. "I'll find it," he said. "When?"

"Eleven o'clock tomorrow morning?"

"I'll be there."

Lorita rose and took a step forward as Law stood up. The top of her head came barely to his shoulder. She looked up at him, her lips parted. "Thank you, Mr. Law," she breathed.

"Call me J.T.," he said in a strangled voice as he breathed in her womanly scent. "Or John Thomas, if you prefer."

"Thank you, John Thomas." She waited.

Law could not help himself. He bent his head until his lips found hers. Her mouth was sweet, her lips soft and yielding.

She pulled away after an eternity and whispered huskily, "You won't regret this, John Thomas." She kissed him again, harder. Then she broke it off. Looking a little flustered, she turned and hurried out.

Law stood there for several minutes, wondering about the whirlwind of lust-inducing, heart-stopping womanhood who had just come into his life. After a while, he lay down to go back to sleep, but it was a long time in coming.

When it did, Law slept away the afternoon and straight through the night. He awoke refreshed, however. He dressed and ate well in the restaurant next door, devouring two small beefsteaks, half a dozen eggs, and two stacks of flapjacks. Three cups of coffee washed it down, then he relaxed with a final cup of Arbuckle's and a thin cigar.

Afterward, he headed toward the seamstress's house. As he walked, he ignored the heat. The prospect not only of spending some time with Lorita Kuykendall this afternoon but also the possibility of bringing Chester Kuykendall to justice allowed him to push the punishing temperature out of his mind. He left his old frock coat with the seamstress to have the bullet hole re- · paired and left clad in his new—and newly altered—garment.

At Wentworth's, he picked up two boxes of shells for the Colts and a half dozen bandannas. He had a shot of whiskey with Alva Wentworth as they each smoked a cigar and chatted. When Law left the store, he considered visiting McCracken, then decided after glancing at his watch that he did not have the time. He strolled to O'Fallon's and brought Toby out of a stall.

"Ought to give that animal more rest, boy-o," O'Fallon said, strolling up. "Critter's been hard used." He looked disapprovingly at Law and breathed old whiskey on the bounty man.

Law turned and stood in front of the horse, one big hand on each side of the buckskin's head. "You been hard used, Toby?" he asked, voice gentle.

The horse nickered softly and bobbed his great head.

Law gave him a lump of sugar from his pocket. "I bet you have, boy," he said. He turned to face O'Fallon. "You're right,

Mr. O'Fallon. He has been purty hard used of late, though not from any mistreatment. Me and Toby here have had us some interestin' adventures the past few days."

"Yeah, well, he should be treated better, boy-o."

Law's eyes narrowed. "Don't you ever accuse me again of ill-treatin' a horse, you old reprobate."

"Aw right, aw right. Don't get your feathers all ruffled up."

Law nodded. "But seein' as how you do seem to care about Toby, I think I'll leave him here with you today. Saddle me that horse Mr. Blackstone was usin'."

O'Fallon scowled as he headed off to do as he had been bidden, wiping snot from his running nose on a hand, which he then cleaned on his filthy pants. Shaking his head, Law put Toby back into the stall. "You rest up, boy," he said.

Soon after, Law tied his coat to the cantle of his saddle, mounted up, and rode out of Big Spring, trying to adjust himself to the gait of the unfamiliar horse. He rode at a good clip, rapidly getting accustomed to the sturdy gray's movement. He decided before long that with a little work, the horse would be a fine animal.

When he judged that he was four miles outside of town, he cut off the road, heading south and west. Within minutes, he spotted the solitary mesquite. It was not a tall tree, but its branches spread considerably. As Law got within a hundred yards of it, he spotted Lorita, and his heart gave an involuntary leap. She stood on this side of the rise's slope, waving to him. He picked up the pace.

When he was twenty yards from the base of the knoll, three men suddenly burst forth, one from each side of the little ridge, the other coming over the top. All were firing as they charged.

CHAPTER 24

LAW FOUGHT TO control the gray, which was not used to such activity, while trying to pull the big Peacemaker. A bullet thudded into his right arm, high, and he dropped the pistol.

"Damn!" he cursed. Despite the pain, he grabbed out the shorter-barreled Colt and fired twice. The man to Law's right went down, falling off his mount in a heap.

Law desperately wished he had Toby under him. The horse could maneuver through a battlefield better on his own than most horses could with direction. Law heeled the gray forward, hoping to mount something of a charge. But before the animal could get moving, two bullets hit it, one in the chest the other in the neck just in front of the saddle.

The horse stumbled forward a couple of steps and then fell. Law managed to jump to the side as the horse went down, keeping his limbs from being trapped under the beast. He scrabbled up to where he was lying at right angles to the horse's belly. He poked his head and gun over the animal's still heaving side. The two remaining men were close, and

Law ducked behind the horse's body, listening to the thwack as several more bullets plowed into the horse—and his saddle.

The men raced by, firing down at him but not even coming close. He rolled over onto his back and snapped off two more shots. He hit nothing. But the next time he fired, he hit one of the men in the side of the head as the two gunmen were turning their mounts.

The last one, whom Law now recognized as Billy Crawford, spurred his horse forward. Law fired off his last round, but missed when a bullet from Crawford's pistol tore a shallow furrow up the length of Law's forearm. "Damn!" Law exclaimed as new pain burned his arm. He dropped the pistol, but picked it up. Holding it in his left hand, he hurriedly began reloading the weapon. It was an effort, considering that his right arm was nearly useless and the blood made everything slippery. As he worked, he kept shifting his glance from what he was doing to the enemy.

The gunman slowed his horse and stopped just yards away. With a devilish grin, he slid off the horse and approached Law on foot. "Well, well, well," he said, stopping inches from Law's boots. "Looks like the famous bounty man J.T. Law ain't so great after all. I knew I'd face you again after you killed Clem in Wentworth's store that time." He sneered. "How's it feel knowin' you're gonna die because you were stupid enough to let some bitch trick you into an ambush, boy?"

"What makes you think I'm gonna die, bub?" Law countered, seething at Lorita's trickery but not wanting to let Crawford see it. He surreptitiously eased back the hammer of the Colt with his left thumb.

"A gunman ain't much good without his gun arm workin'," Crawford said with another sneer. He raised his pistol. "Farewell, Mr. Big-Time Bounty Man."

Law snapped his revolver up and fired three times, punching a trio of bloody holes in the man's chest.

Crawford's eyes widened in surprise, but the look faded almost as quickly as he dropped his gun, staggered back two steps, and crumpled to the ground.

Law pushed himself up. With his right arm hanging straight

down, and the Colt in his left hand, he moved up to the man and loomed over him. "How's it feel to be killed by a one-armed man?" he asked sarcastically.

"Ain't dead yet," Crawford said valiantly, though he knew he would not last long with three lead bullets in his chest.

"Yes, you are." Law lifted the Colt and put a bullet between the man's eyes. He turned to see Lorita racing away astride a horse.

Fighting back the anger at having been duped, Law managed to tie one of his new bandannas around the wound in his upper arm. That was the one bleeding the most. The other was not bad, though it looked ugly. He gingerly reloaded the Colt again and went to get the bigger pistol he had dropped when first shot.

Luckily for him, Crawford's horse had not moved, and Law was able to walk slowly up to it and take the reins. He quick-hobbled the horse and then went to loosen his saddle on the dead gray. He tied a rope around the saddle horn, then un-hobbled the dead man's horse and painfully mounted it. He dallied the rope around the horn and backed the animal up, tugging his saddle from under the dead gray after considerable effort.

Dismounting, he tossed Crawford's gear in the dirt, then took his saddlebags, bedroll, scabbard, rifle, and coat and put them on Crawford's horse. He mounted up and headed toward town, running the horse hard the whole time, in case Lorita had sent other would-be killers after him.

He was in Dr. Hayes's office getting bandaged up when Jess McCracken walked in. "You all right, J.T.?" McCracken asked, looking worried.

"I been better, but I'll live."

"What've you got to say, Doc?" McCracken asked, not wanting to trust his friend's opinion on this.

"He'll be right as rain in a couple of weeks, Sheriff," Hayes said. He helped Law put on a clean shirt taken from his saddlebags, then put his arm in a sling. "Now don't you go gettin' too frisky with that arm for a spell, Mr. Law," he finally said.

Law nodded and slapped his hat on.

"What the hell happened?" McCracken asked as they

walked outside and headed down the street toward Mc-Cracken's office.

Law told him everything, from the meeting with Lorita Kuykendall yesterday to his arrival at the doctor's.

"I told you she was one evil she-wolf," McCracken chided him.

"Yep, you did, Jess. But what you didn't tell me, you son of a bitch, was that she was the finest lookin' female to ever walk the earth. Good goddamn, Jess, I swear, if she had showed me her bosom, I might've gone off and joined her husband's gang."

McCracken managed a chuckle. "She has that effect on a lot of men."

"But not you?"

"Nah, not me, J.T. I'm older than you and have sowed my oats. Besides, I'm married to Lucy Mae, and she's one of the finest women there ever was. Now, was I still single, I ain't sayin' I couldn't be swayed by that woman's charms."

They entered the office, and McCracken dragged out a bottle of whiskey and two glasses. When they had sipped a bit, the sheriff asked, "What're you plannin' to do now, J.T.?"

"Finish what was started here," Law said flatly. "Kuykendall has to pay. I still owe that to Hank Blackstone."

"And Lorita?"

Law ignored the question. He rose and finished off the glass of whiskey. "Thanks for this," he said, tipping the glass at McCracken. "Be seein' you, Jess." He walked out and went straight to Wentworth's. "You got any dynamite, Alva?" he asked the store owner.

"Sure." He looked a little surprised. "How much you need?"

"Half a dozen sticks ought to do."

"I'll make it nine, just in case." He headed into the back of the store and returned with a sack, which he handed to Law. "Anything else, J.T.?"

Law shook his head. He paid the man and, carrying the bag, headed outside and down to the livery. O'Fallon knew better than to argue when Law told him to take the saddle off the dead man's horse and put it on Toby. O'Fallon didn't even say anything when Law asked him to help adjust the stirrups. Hanging the bag of dynamite over the saddle horn, Law rode out.

As he neared the ranch, Law saw two men riding toward him. He pulled his right arm out of the sling, gingerly pulled out his pistol and transferred it to his left hand before he returned his arm to the sling and then took the reins in that hand. The action left him sweating even more than the heat did.

When the two riders slowly approached him, Law could see they did not have the look of hired guns about them. Still, he cocked the Colt and sat with it resting on his thigh. "You boys work for Kuykendall?" he asked when the young men stopped.

One nodded, but hastily said, "We're just cowpunchers, mister. Not hired guns."

Law believed him. "How many guns does he have left out there?"

"None," the same man said. At Law's look of disbelief, he added, "They all took off early this afternoon. Me and Sim here, we were in the bunkhouse when Mrs. Kuykendall"—his eyes filled briefly with a lustful desire—"come ridin' back to the house hell-bent for leather. There was a heap of shoutin' from inside the house, then Mr. Kuykendall called in some of the men. There was more hollerin', then the hired guns come out, went to their bunkhouses. Not ten minutes later, the two bunkhouses those men used was empty. Mr. and Mrs. Kuykendall started packin' a wagon. We figured we'd head on into Big Spring and see about findin' new work if the boss wasn't gonna be around no more."

"Obliged for the information, boys," Law said. He rode off, glancing over his shoulder occasionally, but the two riders kept moving away from him. He finally uncocked the Colt, but instead of trying to get it back into the holster at his right hip, which would spark a new round of pain, he simply stuck it into his waistband.

When he came into sight of the ranch buildings, Law lit a cigar. He rode straight in, certain the two cowmen had been telling the truth, since the place had an eerie emptiness and quiet about it. Just in case, though, he lit sticks of dynamite and tossed a couple of them into each of the two bunkhouses used by Kuykendall's gunmen. The blasts shattered the structures, but no one came out.

Law stopped at the house and dismounted. With the cocked pistol in his left hand, he entered the place and looked around. He found no one, and it looked as if it had been ransacked. He put the gun back into his waistband and went outside, where he looked around. In moments he found tracks of a loaded wagon heading west. He mounted Toby and followed at a good pace. He figured Kuykendall couldn't be too far ahead.

He was right. In less than an hour, as he topped a rise, he saw a wagon ahead. Law smiled grimly and turned to the right. He rode hard for half a mile, swung back west for twice that, and then south a bit. He stopped and waited, facing east. In minutes, the wagon came lumbering into view.

Kuykendall tried to hide his surprise when he saw who the rider waiting for him was.

"This is the end of the trail for you, Kuykendall," Law said. "You can either come along peaceably back to Big Spring or . . ."

"Or what?" Kuykendall asked with a sneer. He pushed the brake handle, then wrapped the lines around it. He jumped down from the wagon and tugged off his coat, revealing the brace of Remingtons at his hips. "What're you gonna do, Law? I don't figure you're much of a threat with a broken gun arm."

Law dismounted and faced the man with the frizzy red hair, muttonchops, and mustache. "Where's the missus?" he asked. "She run out on you, too, like your hired guns?"

Kuykendall laughed. "She left the Double Bar K before I did. She'll be waitin' a few miles up the road for me." He leered. "She really flummoxed you, boy, didn't she. Goddamn, I couldn't believe she pulled the wool over your eyes so easy."

Rage burned in Law's chest, but he forced himself not to show it. "What's it gonna be, Kuykendall?"

"It's gonna be your death, bounty man." Both hands darted for pistols.

Law was a bit slower in pulling the Colt from his waistband, but even with his left hand, a pistol was a natural extension of him. Three bullets ripped into Kuykendall—chest, throat, and head. He crumpled like a leaking sack of grain.

Despite his injured arm, Law managed to lift Kuykendall into the back of his wagon. He was lucky the dead man was thin, even if he was tall. Law tied Toby to the back of the wagon, then climbed aboard and got the thing moving.

LAW FELT A jolt of pleasure when he saw the surprise on Lorita's face as she realized it was he driving the wagon instead of her husband. He felt a jolt of another kind as the surprise faded and her natural sultriness beamed forth. Damn, she was a beautiful woman, he thought. It helped a little, though, that she was dressed in a man's shirt and trousers for traveling.

"It's over, Lorita," Law said as he stepped down from the wagon.

"Where's Chester?" she asked, suddenly looking frightened.

"Back of the wagon," Law said flatly, chucking a thumb over his shoulder.

Lorita walked away from her horse and looked in the wagon bed. When she turned to face Law again, there was real grief in her eyes.

"Why'd you kill him?" she asked, trying to regain her composure.

"He drew down on me. Figured that since one arm is out of commission that he could take me. He was wrong." He paused, fighting back the anger. In some ways he wanted to kill her right where she stood for the way she had used him, setting him up to be killed. But killing women was not his way. He hated to admit it, but her beauty and the lust he still harbored for her made him even more reluctant to do so. Still, she had to face justice, one way or the other.

Casting aside her grief, she sashayed up close to him, letting him feel her heat, letting her beauty wash over him, letting her womanly scent cover him.

It was difficult, but he resisted. "It ain't gonna work this time, Mrs. Kuykendall," he said softly. "I may be a damn fool most times, like most men, but I'm on to your ways. In your own way, you're as devilish as your late husband was."

"And I thought you were a real man," she spat, stepping back from him. The sneer drained her face of much of its beauty. "But you're not. You're just another foolish man. Big and tough with a gun in your hand, but stupid as an ox around a woman. And to think I almost believed in your reputation. Whoo, big, bad bounty man. Hah! Couldn't even keep that loudmouthed farm boy alive."

His rapidly rising anger was making it all the easier to resist her.

"A real man would've took me yesterday right then and there. I thought maybe I was losin' my touch when you didn't, but now I realize it was just because you ain't much of a man. . . ."

Law let her go on for a little. He had a great urge to just wallop her, but that was against his nature, too. Finally, he had had enough, however, and he bellowed, "Shut your flappin' goddamn hole, or I will slap it shut for you!"

The words stopped, though her mouth gaped, and her eyes were huge and round.

"I ought to just hang you," he said more calmly, enjoying the real fear in her face. "But there ain't no trees hereabouts." He smiled savagely. "But I am takin' you back to Big Spring, where, I hope, you will face justice."

"I won't go," Lorita said, still frightened, but too used to having her way to give up just yet.

"Yes, you will." His tone left no doubt to the veracity of his words. "Now, you can go sitting up in the wagon next to me, or I can truss you up like a Christmas goose and toss you in the back with your late, unlamented husband."

"You wouldn't dare."

His look told her differently.

"All right," she said, shoulders sagging. She was certain that she could change his mind as they traveled.

He tied her horse to the wagon next to Toby, then they climbed onto the wagon seat, Lorita on his left, away from his injured arm. She glanced at the pistol butt swinging in the shoulder holster so close to her.

"Don't even consider it," he said as he turned the wagon.

As they rode, she edged closer and closer to him, until she was pressed right against his side. He didn't mind, but he was not going to let himself be seduced by her. He figured it would serve her well to have her think she was going to change his ways, only to be disappointed.

Eventually, she placed a hand on his thigh, then inched it toward his manhood. She almost made it when he said, "You don't move your hand, I'll break your fingers."

The hand withdrew, and she moved away from him a little, sitting stiffly as darkness approached. As full darkness arrived, she moved a little closer to him and soon lay her head on his shoulder. He was about to protest, then realized she had fallen asleep.

They arrived in Big Spring just after dawn and stopped at the sheriff's office. McCracken stepped outside, not surprised at all by what he saw. Law and McCracken escorted Lorita inside, where the sheriff apologetically put her in a cell in back. She screeched and hollered, but McCracken shut the door separating the cells from the main office, cutting off most of her noise. Once more he broke out the whiskey and two glasses, then made a small, silent toast. They clinked glasses and drank a bit.

"You know, J.T.," McCracken said, "I doubt much will happen to her. She's a woman, and she's not known to have taken part in any of the crimes with her husband. I don't know what to charge her with."

"Settin' me up to be killed," Law snapped.

"Jury might buy that. Might not, though."

"I should've hanged her myself when I found her," Law growled. "I'd wager big money that I ain't the first man she's ever seduced into getting himself bushwhacked. It's a damn good bet, though, that I'm the first one ever lived through it."

Law set his glass down. With a sick feeling at his failures, Law walked outside, mounted Toby, and rode out of Big Spring.